THE YOUNG WAN

THE YOUNG WAN

An Agnes Browne Novel

Brendan O'Carroll

VIKING

VIKING
Published by the Penguin Group
Penguin Putnam Inc., 375 Hudson Street,
New York, New York 10014, U.S.A.
Penguin Books Ltd, 80 Strand,
London WC2R oRL, England
Penguin Books Australia Ltd, 250 Camberwell Road, Camberwell,
Victoria 3124, Australia
Penguin Books Canada Ltd, 10 Alcorn Avenue,
Toronto, Ontario, Canada M4V 3B2
Penguin Books India (P) Ltd, 11 Community Centre, Panchsheel Park,
New Delhi – 110 017, India
Penguin Books (N.Z.) Ltd, Cnr Rosedale and Airborne Roads, Albany,
Auckland, New Zealand
Penguin Books (South Africa) (Pty) Ltd, 24 Sturdee Avenue, Rosebank,
Johannesburg 2196, South Africa

Penguin Books Ltd, Registered Offices:
Harmondsworth, Middlesex, England

First published in 2003 by Viking Penguin,
a member of Penguin Putnam Inc.

1   3   5   7   9   10   8   6   4   2

PUBLISHER'S NOTE
This is a work of fiction. Names, characters, places, and incidents either are the product
of the author's imagination or are used fictitiously, and any resemblance to actual per-
sons, living or dead, business establishments, events, or locales is entirely coincidental.

LIBRARY OF CONGRESS CATALOGING IN PUBLICATION DATA
O'Carroll, Brendan, date.
The young wan : an Agnes Browne novel / Brendan O'Carroll.
p.   cm.
ISBN 0-670-03114-3
1. Browne, Agnes (Fictitious character)—Fiction.   2. Dublin (Ireland)—Fiction.
3. Young women—Fiction.   I. Title
PR6065.C36 Y68 2003
823.914—dc21   2002033092

This book is printed on acid-free paper. ∞

Printed in the United States of America
Set in Goudy   Designed by Francesca Belanger

It is with all the love in my heart
and my belief in their future
that I dedicate this book
to

my son
Eric O'Carroll

and

my goddaughter
Julia Grace Nolan

❧

Acknowledgments

I WOULD LIKE TO SAY THANK YOU and some words to the people
who have prepared me for takeoff and continue to make me fly.

Billy Flood, for his belief. You were more than a teacher, you are
an inspiration.

Fiona O'Carroll, my daughter. When I took you in my arms for
the first time, you were the most beautiful baby I had ever seen.
Nothing in the last twenty-one years has changed my mind. Daddy
loves you, Princess.

Danny O'Carroll, my eldest son. If I had a wish to grant those
people I love, it would be that they have a son like you.

Eric O'Carroll, my youngest son. You make me laugh, and you
fill my life with the wonders of your fantastic imagination. I love
you so much I could burst.

Jenny Gibney, my life and love partner. The vault within which
my fragile heart is safe.

Rory Cowan, to whom I dedicated my last book. I'm sorry I hurt
you. Thank you for forgiving me.

Fiona Gowland, my sister. You have no idea how proud I am to
point you out and tell those in my company *that* is my sister.

Mike Nolan, my friend, my ally, my brother.

Martin Delany, my friend. Life really is like a box of chocolates,
Martin. Don't go on a diet!

Paddy Houlihan. All right, horse? If God had granted me the grace of another child, I would wish it were you.

Annette Dolan, my friend. My life would have been so much the poorer over the last ten years had God not sent you to me.

Clyde Carroll, my friend. Your future is in your hands. I delight in being the vehicle if you are a careful driver.

Conor Brett, my friend. You have a unique talent, to come through every time you're asked. Thank you.

Fiona Gibney, my friend. Who lost Saturdays, Sundays, and sleep to help me over the line.

John Bond, who straightened out my life and taught me two plus two is four.

Evelyn Conway. To this day I still do not know. But I shall never forget the contribution your being in my life has meant to my success. Never.

Rosemary Ahern, my friend. I regret you could not finish what you started, but you left me in good hands. Really good.

Clare Ferraro. The boss. You, just you alone, you package of positive energy, epitomize everything that is great about New York. Its strength, its open-arm welcome for anyone and everyone, your belief in tomorrow, and in me.

And finally . . .

Karen Murphy. Without doubt the finest editor I have ever had. You massaged this book out of me, convinced me I had a voice, and gently kicked me over every obstacle. I hope I have not let you down.

God bless you all.

Brendan

Introduction

WHEN I WAS A CHILD my mother, Maureen, would dress me for school and then stand back to check me over. There wasn't a lot to check. The L-shaped rip in my shoulder she had mended with her famous "invisible stitching," which was about as invisible as the job done on Frankenstein's monster's forehead. The holes that had been in the elbows of my woolen jumper she had "darned," a dying if not dead skill. She was a beautiful darner and used a basket-weave stitch. This was obvious, for the navy-blue darning wool stood out on the elbows of my green jumper, as it did on my gray socks. These socks were protected from the holes in the soles of my shoes by the piece of linoleum she had inserted. The soles may have been worn through, but the brogues shone from the polishing she had given them. So there I stood, my clothes held together by my mother's skill, but spotlessly clean. My shoes sealed by a piece of somebody's old flooring, but shining, and me smelling of the Sunlight carbolic soap with which she had earlier washed me from head to toe. The raggle-taggle schoolboy. Taking all of this into account, her last words to me each morning were all the more astounding. She would smile, pinch my cheek, and, looking me straight in the eyes, say, "Brendan you can be anything you want to be; you, my son, can do anything."

I left schooling at twelve years of age. My mother left me one morning when I was twenty-eight. She took my son Danny, then just ten months old, for a mid-morning nap. He fell asleep, and so did she. I cannot tell you in just this one page of how wonderful a woman she was, but I promise that one day I will. The only one of my three children that really knew her was my daughter, Fiona, who adored her, and in Fiona I see so much of my mother that it warms me.

My mother is not nor was not Agnes Browne. Yet they shared something in common that I believe to be a trait unique to women. And it is this—that even while their world is falling apart around their ears they truly can still believe that their dreams will come true.

One morning I questioned my mother's promise to me. She said her usual "You can be anything you want to be . . ." line, and I asked her, "Mammy, can I fly?" She smiled and said, "Sure you can. Just put your arms out, work hard, and wait, and I promise you, someday you will fly." When she died I was a waiter. Since her death I have written five novels, four stage plays, two screenplays, hosted my own television series, acted in eight movies, and performed live comedy to over one million people on three continents. She never got to see any of this. At the end of each live show, when the audience stand, cheer, and applaud, it is a wonderful feeling, and I love it. The audience smile and cheer and they cannot hear me say quietly to the uplifting air, *"Look, Mammy, I'm flying."*

Brendan O'Carroll
Dublin, 2002

THE YOUNG WAN

PROLOGUE

The parish of St. Jarlath occupies a northeastern portion of Dublin City Centre. Stretching from the banks of the river Liffey north to Summerhill, and from Fairview Park, on the east coast, westward to Gardiner Street, just short of the city's premier thoroughfare, O'Connell Street. The main focus of the parish, however, is the eight square blocks of tenement buildings that surround St. Jarlath's Church itself. This small area within the parish is known to all who live there as the Jarro.

If there were any single thing one could point to that would unite the memories of all of the thousands of people who had been born, reared, and starved in the Jarro, it would be the noise. The only change over the years has been the types and the sources, but the level has stayed the same.

The noise of the Jarro is built of three layers. The background noise is a symphony of transport. Once it had been only the *clip-clop* and rattle of horses' carriages along with the low rumble of handcarts of every shape and size as they crisscrossed the cobbled streets. The middle-ground noise has *always* been children. Screaming, crying, playing, kicking, and laughing children. Within the Jarro children outnumber adults by four to one. The sound of children covers the area like a blanket. And yet, still, like a colony of sea lions, a Dublin mother could hear "one of her own" from two blocks away. It is this talent that gives us the foreground noise, the

Dublin woman's voice. It can pierce a steel door at twenty paces. Women of the Jarro would exchange the most intimate details of their lives, or better still someone else's, in conversations across the street, from window to window, at a piercing level, and with no effort at all. These conversations or gossip would probably make no sense to an outsider listening in, but to these hardworking, tough women, they did, and that's all that mattered. Over the noise of the streets and screaming kids, they can be heard.

"See that young wan O'Brien got the brush-off from her boyfriend," one would call to another.

"I heard that all right, what happened there?" comes the reply.

"'E said he wouldn't marry a girl what's not a virgin," is explained. A short silence follows this piece of news.

"And is she a virgin?" the question would come at a scream.

"No, not yet," is delivered with authority. Amazingly, considering that this conversation is taking place at screaming level, across a street, should a third voice join in she would be told to mind her own business.

So these, then, are the sounds of the Jarro, a tenement area on Dublin's Northside crammed with working-class and unemployed people and their large families. The four-story red brick buildings, once regal and grand, were now old and unkempt, damp and dreary. The streets dirty and dark, shrouded in a pall of smoke from the thousands of coal or peat fires burning in the buildings. And yet there is so much more to the Jarro than its streets and its buildings. For through the smoke there is music and song. Within these buildings there is genuine community. Sharing, caring community. Every day on these streets young boys dream of becoming millionaires and young girls dream of marrying handsome princes (not from the Jarro). Within this cramped, smoky, damp Jarro live the dreams of five thousand people. And laughter. At every chance there is laughter. There is magic here. It may not be the pixie-dust, float-on-a-cloud, fairies-at-the-bottom-of-the-garden kind, but take my word, in the Jarro there *is* magic.

The Jarro, Dublin
July 17, 1954

This morning, at 5:15 a.m., the blood-red sun began to peek over the copper dome of the Customs House building. Its beautiful July rising sent a streak of amber light through the window of Agnes Reddin's bedroom. Morning. The day had arrived. Not just any day, but *the* day. This day, at 4 p.m., Agnes Reddin would make the short journey to St. Jarlath's Church. She would enter the church a nineteen-year-old "young wan" and the next time she stood on its steps, which would hopefully be about thirty minutes later, she would be a woman. To be known to all from this day hence as

Mrs. Agnes Browne.

Slowly the sunlight crept along Agnes' bed until it found her beautiful young, smiling face. Agnes had been awake for some time. She was sitting upright in the bed. Thinking, as you do on such auspicious days. Beside her this morning lay her best friend and maid of honor, Marion Monks, sleeping. Marion was neither a maid nor had she displayed any honor for the last hour or so. For Agnes' thinking had been punctuated by a regular cycle of snoring, grunting, and farting from her sleeping friend. Agnes smiled at the crumpled, tiny figure of her friend, at the same time tucking the blankets, tightly sealing herself from the deadly *thrummmp* of the fart that Agnes knew was due any moment. It arrived. Marion smiled, rubbed her nose roughly, and with a grunt returned to a steady snore.

Agnes and Marion were as different as chalk and cheese. Agnes was blessed with her father's dark looks and raven hair, and, along with the slim figure of her mother, she was a stunning-looking girl. Marion, on the other hand, was just four feet eight inches tall and shaped like a barrel. She had a round face, tiny gray dots for eyes, and on her chin sported three brown moles. Each of the three moles had a tuft of hair growing from it, and when Marion smiled, which she did often, the moles would merge to make a little goatee beard. The two girls had been friends since childhood. Their lives entwined like a fisherman's rope and the bond between them just as strong.

Agnes slowly slid from the bed, trying not to waken Marion, for whom a sleep beyond 5 a.m. was a luxury. Most mornings at this time the two young women would be already up. They would be at the fruit-and-vegetable wholesale markets on Green Street, ordering their stock for the day. Not today. Agnes quietly left the room.

The other bedroom was occupied by Agnes' mother, Connie, who at that moment was sitting in an identical pose to the one Agnes had just abandoned, upright in bed. She had not woken at 5 a.m., for she had not slept since returning to bed earlier. Instead she had sat in her pose and stayed awake. Thinking! As you do on such auspicious days as wedding days. However, where the daughter Agnes was thinking about the future, the mother's thoughts were firmly rooted in the past, along with her mind. Although she was only fifty-seven years old, Agnes' mother, Connie, looked more in her seventies. Her early dementia and illnesses had taken their toll, and in a role reversal Agnes had long ago become her mother's mother. The dementia would come and go. On some occasions Agnes' mother became quite clear and rational, allowing Agnes to revisit the intelligent woman that her mother once was. Mostly, though, Connie was in a different place, a little closer to God than the rest of us. Yet she would slip in and out, and so rapidly sometimes only Agnes would see the flashes. Agnes has always believed that this had been mostly caused by the trauma of the death of

Agnes' father. For, despite his faults, and there were many, Bosco Reddin had been so deeply loved by his wife, Connie.

As Agnes passed her mother's bedroom door, she stopped and listened. Her mother was singing. Very quietly, but singing. Agnes recognized the song. *"I could show the world how to smile, make it seem happy, just for a while, I could turn the gray skies to blue, if I had you."* It was her father's song. He would sing it when he burst through the door, late home and drunk. When he knew he was in trouble. It was not very often her father got drunk. But when he did he would sing this song to his "three lovely lassies." Agnes and her younger sister, Dolly, little girls then, would blush and titter with laughter. Mammy would call him a drunken fool and pretend to be angry. She probably was at first, but he would just keep singing the song until she smiled.

Agnes felt the teardrop on the back of her hand. She moved on to the living room. Although it was July and sunny outside, the sitting room was chilly, so Agnes decided to light a fire, just to warm the room a bit. She put on her dressing gown and left the flat with the scuttle bucket to fetch coal from the coal hole in the basement.

Soon the fire was lighting and the room was warm. Agnes ran the tap and dragged out the three large pots she would use to boil the water for her bath. As the first one was filling slowly, Agnes went back to the bedroom.

"Marion," she called gently as she woke her maid of honor. "Move it, come on, we have a lot to do today."

"I'm up, I'm up!" answered Marion.

"You're not up, now come on, Marion." Agnes was at the bottom of the bed and tickled Marion's foot as she said this. Marion jumped.

"Fuck off or I'll kill you, Agnes."

"Get up, then, come on!" Agnes was getting annoyed, just a little.

"I am. Go on, put the kettle on or something." Marion sat up. She looked like the wreck of the *Hesperus*.

Agnes heaved the last of the three large pots of water up onto the gas stove. She wiped her hands in the tea towel and lit a match. Turning the gas knobs in turn, she poked a lighted match beneath each pot, and as she did the jets popped into life.

"What the fuck are you cooking at this hour of the morning?" asked a groggy Marion. Agnes jumped.

"Jesus, Marion, you frightened the life out of me."

"What time is it?" Marion asked, as she sat and began pulling on a canvas slipper.

"Half past eight," Agnes answered as she carried on with her business.

"*What?* Half past eight, I didn't get up this early for me own fucking wedding!" Marion was dismayed, realizing she'd not been to bed until 3:45 a.m. Agnes laughed.

"Shut up, you, and mind your language. Me mammy's awake," Agnes scolded.

"Like your mammy'd know? She's probably in there raping Napoleon." Marion pulled on the other slipper.

"Ah, Marion, shush, that's not nice," Agnes admonished Marion, but she giggled as she did so. As Agnes took a sip from her tea, Marion called out toward the mammy's bedroom door.

"Go on, Mrs. Reddin, pull the knob off'a him!" They roared with laughter.

Agnes began to choke with the laughter. She put the tea mug down awkwardly and was spluttering and laughing so much that tea was dripping from her nostrils. Marion began to laugh even harder now and threw herself on the floor and began writhing and moaning.

"Come on, Boneypart, ya good thing—show me your cannon-balls."

Agnes was bent double laughing. She flung herself on top of Marion, trying to cover Marion's mouth with her hand. In a repeat of the previous night's playing, the two girls wrestled around on the floor for a full three minutes. When they stopped, they again lay on the floor beside each other, breathless and exhausted. They lay on their backs. Agnes held on to Marion's hand.

"Jesus, I'm getting married," Agnes softly said.

"Yeh," her friend answered.

Both their heads turned to the wedding dress hanging there.

"Do you remember the last time you wore a white dress?" Marion asked. They both smiled a knowing smile and spoke simultaneously.

"Holy Communion class." Now they cried with laughter again.

"Do you remember?" Marion asked.

"Will I ever forget . . ."

It was the day they had become friends, forever friends.

CHAPTER ONE

Blessed Heart Girls National School
The Jarro, February 1940

It is the line that all Catholics get to say just once in their life-
time. Conducted in their rhythm by Sister Concepta Pius, the
forty-four young little girls in the Communion class sang out
the line in unison, like a tiny girls' choir.

"Bless me, Father, for I have sinned. This is my *first* confession,"
they sang. Although the little girls were still three years from having
to say this in a real confessional, in the Blessed Heart School, the nuns
believed it was never too early to prepare for communion with God.

"Well done, my little angels." Sister Concepta Pius smiled.
"Now, is everybody clear on that?" The nun's squinting eyes
scanned the room.

As usual there was just one hand in the air, and as usual it was
the hand of Marion Delany. Sister Concepta raised her eyes slowly
to heaven and asked, "Yes, Marion?"

Marion Delany stood, but you could hardly notice. Marion Delany was the tiniest girl in the class, and yet at seven years of age she
was two years older than the rest of the girls. It was not that Marion
had been held back a couple of years in school because of any learning difficulty. The fact was that, until she was seven years of age,
Marion Delany had never attended school. The reason for this is
simple, yet complicated, as Marion's mother tried to explain to the
officer from the Department of Education who called to her home.
The officer had been sent there when the department realized that

a child from the Birth Register seven years previously had yet to come on to the School Register, two years after she should have. It was all to do with public transport, Marion's mother tried to explain. You see, in Dublin, no child four years or younger had to pay any fare to travel on public transport. Now, the Delany family was made up of two boys and eight girls. The girls ranged in age from four years of age to fourteen years of age, and the truth is that between the four-year-old and the fourteen-year-old the height difference was barely noticeable. When traveling with their mother on public transport, the Delany children were always schooled that if a bus conductor should ask them what age they were they should say "four." With so many daughters and after so many trips, Mrs. Delany simply *forgot* what age each of her children was. If anybody asked any Delany girl what age she was, the immediate answer would be "four." And, truthfully, as Marion stood in the aisle of the classroom that morning with her hand in the air, she really looked like she could just be little more than four.

"You have a question, Marion Delany?" the nun asked for the twentieth time that day, for Marion always had a question. Marion took a deep breath and asked her question.

"Sister, do cats and dogs have souls?" she asked.

"No, Marion. Sit down," Sister Concepta answered. Marion didn't sit.

"Not even teensy-weensy little souls, like just this size?" And she held her two fingers just slightly apart.

"Marion, shut up and sit down," Sister Concepta simply answered, and Marion sat down. Sister Concepta now continued with the lesson.

"Once you have spoken these words—'Bless me, Father, for I have sinned. This is my first confession'—God will open His heart and carry the weight of your sins for you for the rest of your life." She smiled.

Marion Delany's hand went up. Marion didn't stand this time or wait to be asked, she simply blurted out the question.

"Is a sin heavy, Sister?"

"Shut up, Marion."

"Yes, Sister."

Sister Concepta carried on to a hushed classroom: "This is God's lesson in forgiveness. He opens His heart and forgives you all your sins, as you must forgive others theirs. God tells you in the Bible that, if someone slaps you on the cheek, what do you do?"

"Kick him in the balls." The answer from the tiny voice was perfectly timed.

"Who said that?" Sister Concepta nearly screamed.

Every other girl in the class knew it was Marion Delany, but they were from the Jarro, and even at five years of age you knew that nobody likes a snitch. Yet the honor among the girls was wasted.

"I did," came Marion's tiny voice. She stood with her hand in the air. "That's what my dad said you do if somebody slaps you, you kick him in the balls."

Sister Concepta took two long strides and was standing in front of Marion, towering over the little girl. Marion had a round, chubby body with a round head and an ever-present smile. Marion's beaming smile slowly disappeared as the great dark figure of the nun scowled down at her.

"Marion Delany, if I ever hear such language in this class again I'll . . . I'll . . ." She dragged Marion to the front of the class. She shoved her hand beneath her tunic, and when her hand reappeared it held a leather strap.

"Hold out your hand!" Sister Concepta screamed at the terrified little girl.

Marion knew what was coming. Slowly she stretched out her right arm and opened her palm. She stood there looking like a tiny pink snowman with one arm. In her seat Agnes closed her eyes. She couldn't look. Marion received four slaps, one for each word. Sister Concepta spoke:

"Turn . . . *slap* . . . the . . . *slap* . . . other . . . *slap* . . . cheek . . . *slap*."

Following the fourth slap, Sister Concepta put her hands on her hips and screamed at Marion, "Do you understand that, girl?"

The little girl was biting her bottom lip. Two rivulets ran down her cheeks, but she managed to nod her head furiously. Just at that moment the school bell sounded for the mid-morning break, bringing to a close for now Marion Delany's lesson in forgiveness.

At the "little break," Agnes went looking for Marion in the schoolyard. Agnes was fascinated by this tiny girl. The schoolyard was not a big one, and Agnes soon saw Marion standing alone at the railings that surrounded the yard. They were old Victorian rails painted black, with each upward bar topped with an arrowhead, giving the impression of a prison yard more than a schoolyard. This impression was reinforced when Agnes found Marion, for she was standing with each of her pudgy little hands holding a bar and her face wedged streetward between two more bars. Agnes approached her cautiously. After the beating she had seen the girl take in class, Agnes expected that Marion was having a weep. When Agnes spoke she spoke to Marion's back.

"Are you all right?" Agnes said softly. Marion turned to her with an unexpected beaming smile. "Yeh, didn't hurt," but Agnes knew it did, and she knew Marion was using the cold metal bars to cool her thrashed hands. Without any bother, Marion flew straight into conversation with Agnes, and as Agnes was to learn, this was Marion's way.

"You're the prettiest girl in the class," Marion said simply to Agnes.

"What?"

"You. The prettiest. Everybody says so, and I'm the ugliest."

"No, you're not," Agnes said.

"Who's uglier, then? Come on, who's uglier than me?" Marion asked. She spoke only in a matter-of-fact tone—no self-pity, just the facts. Agnes was stuck for a reply. "See, I told you. It doesn't matter, 'cause I have a job and I'm going to marry a man that sells insurance. My mother says that they'd go with anyone. Who are you going to marry?" Agnes was breathless just trying to listen to this conversation.

"What? I don't know who I'm going to marry," Agnes stammered out.

"You should marry, eh, an airline pilot. They like pretty girls, you could fly anywhere you like, and they give you chewing gum as well, as much as you want, I seen it on the pictures."

The end of break bell sounded, and Agnes looked over to the school doorway; the various class groups were getting into line to march back into class. She turned back to Marion.

"We better go in," Agnes said and extended her hand. "Come on."

"Nah, you go on, I'm going to work." Marion began to climb the railings.

"But Sister Conception will miss you." Agnes was aghast.

"I don't care." Marion was now on the other side of the rails. "See ya."

"But she'll slap you tomorrow for this." Agnes was panicking now. Marion began to trot away, calling over her shoulder, "She'll slap me anyway, see ya." And she was gone. Agnes returned to the class, but thought of nothing else for the afternoon except this girl who seemed to have no fear. That's what Agnes wanted, what every child wants more than anything else. Just to be not afraid. Within days the two girls were friends. Within weeks they were inseparable, and within months Agnes Reddin was not afraid. They did everything together, growing to have a great influence on each other. Marion began to spend more time at school, and Agnes became more and more unafraid. Incredibly, they would manage to make it through their childhood and teens without ever falling out, as children usually do.

Now, years later, as they lay on the floor holding hands, they wore each other's friendship like a second skin. They lay there breathless and smiling, looking up at *the dress*.

"You're going to go through with it, aren't you? You're determined to wear that dress," Marion said.

"Uh-huh," Agnes confirmed.

"You're a stubborn bitch, do you know that?" Marion half sat as she said this.

"Not stubborn, Marion, I just know what's right, and this is right. It's a stupid rule made by stupid people," Agnes said, stubbornly.

"Made by the Pope," Marion exclaimed.

"Well, so what? What would he know about marriage anyway? If you don't play the game, don't make the rules. That's what I say!" And they both laughed again.

Agnes' rebellious stand was typical of her. She did not lick it from the ground, it was in her genes. It stretched back before she was born to a time when making a stand for what you thought was "right" could cost you your life.

CHAPTER TWO

Dublin
February 23, 1921

Constance Parker-Willis would not recall it for a long time, but her initial encounter with Bosco Reddin had been a traumatic one.

The Parker-Willis family had been casting iron in Dublin since 1801. Constance's father, Geoffrey Parker-Willis, had inherited the foundry from his grandfather, when his own father, an officer in the Light Brigade, had been killed in the Boer War. Always a successful business, the foundry really boomed for Geoffrey with the coming of the Great War, when output and profits soared. War had been good to Geoffrey. He married Julia Cornwell, a timid woman who bore him four daughters.

By 1921, Constance, the eldest of these girls, and nearly twenty-five years of age, was the only Parker-Willis girl who actually worked. Constance had taken a great interest in the foundry from early, and with no son to follow him and two of Constance's three younger sisters married off, with the third about to be, Geoffrey decided to allow Constance to work in the accounting room of the foundry. Constance loved working there. The noise and the heat, the constant explosions of molten droplets hopping across the foundry floor, and the clanking of machinery, were so far removed from the boring world of high society in which her three sisters mixed as to be music to Constance's ears. The foundry was situated on Misery Hill, on Dublin's south docks. The foundry cannot take credit for the street name; rather, it was named Misery Hill in the seventeenth century, when the area was a leper colony.

That cold February day in 1921, Constance had been working in the foundry and was just closing up the accounting rooms for the day when she heard what she thought might be gunfire. The sound of it seemed to be coming from the far side of the river Liffey. The north side.

The one-legged man was spitting at the Tans as they dragged him from the small terraced house. The officer in charge of these bedraggled British militiamen was drunk. He screamed at the soldiers: "Hit the old beggar a few thumps, that'll quieten the Fenian bastard." They did, across the mouth, and with such force that the old man's top and bottom lips burst simultaneously. For a moment the man lay quiet on the cobbles.

"Toss him in the truck," barked the officer. Two of the soldiers bent and turned the body of the old man over.

"He's dead, sir," one of them pronounced.

"Like fuck I am," the dead man screeched and covered the soldier with now scarlet spit.

"You fucking rebel bastard," screamed the Tan. He began to beat the old man with the butt of his rifle. Two more soldiers now tried to drag the old man toward the rear of the truck; all the while the first one kept beating on him. In the back of the truck some other soldiers were laughing and jeering at the beater.

"Hey, Corporal Oliver, having trouble with the prisoner? Lucky he ain't got two legs, he'd be downright dangerous," one called, and the others gave a bawdy laugh.

"Piss off, you wankers," Oliver called back, and now beat harder on the old man.

The boy seemed to come from out of nowhere. One moment the soldiers had a clear way to the back of the truck, the next there was a young black-haired tan-skinned boy standing in front of them. The boy, Bosco Reddin, although just fourteen years old, was big enough to look eighteen. Bosco held a claw hammer in his right hand and a short, pointed saddler's knife in his left. Before the first soldier had a chance to make out the hammer in the boy's hand, it as buried in the man's forehead. The soldier collapsed straight down. The second soldier dropped the old man and opened his mouth to scream while scrambling with his rifle. Too late. The swing of the hammer came in an arc and caught him in the temple. His left eye burst and he began to topple over. Before the second soldier had hit the ground, Corporal Oliver had the wooden butt of a saddler's knife sticking from his throat and blood pouring from his mouth. The boy bent over the old man.

"Daddy? I'm here, Daddy, can you hear me?" He sobbed. The old man opened his eyes. He touched the boy on the cheek.

"Run, Bosco. Run, son," were the old man's only words.

All of this happened in seconds. Soldiers were now pouring from the back of the truck. Rifles were cocked, and they jostled each other to get the space to extend their Brownings into a firing position. Young Bosco Reddin rolled under the truck. The soldiers now fell over themselves trying to get to the other side. But Bosco rolled just halfway, then came out the side he had entered and ran. It took a couple of seconds before the soldiers realized that Bosco was no longer under the truck.

"There he is!" called one, pointing down the street.

Bosco was running hard down the street toward the red brick wall that made his street a dead end. The wall was just six feet high, and Bosco had been vaulting it since he turned twelve years of age, two years ago. The wall was thirty yards from Bosco when the first volley of shots ricocheted well to his left side and behind him. Bosco knew they would adjust their aim to the right, so instinctively he darted to his left. He was correct. The next volley spat pieces of stone up on his right, but now the shots were abreast and ahead of him. Just ten yards to go. *Bang,* the next salvo came, and one bullet passed so close to Bosco's ear that he heard it actually *crack* as it broke the air. The soldiers were shooting at will, and the officer was screaming at them. Bullets were whizzing in all directions. Windows were being shattered, even roof tiles were being damaged by errant ricochets. Bosco's focus now narrowed to a single point. The red brick wall. From behind broken windows and in half-opened doorways he could hear the cries of encouragement from his neighbors.

"Run, Bosco. Run, son." A woman's voice.

Amazingly, he passed one very old man who was standing outside his front door propped up by a well-used hawthorn walking stick. Bullets were pinging all about the old codger, but he was impervious to them. As Bosco came abreast of the man he waved his stick.

"Don't let the bastards get you, lad. Run, Bosco, run."

Bosco ran. He reached the red brick wall. In one swift, smooth move he sprang from the ground, threw his hands to the top of the wall, and pulled his body up. Just as he was clear of the top of the wall, Bosco saw some splinters of red brick shoot up, and he felt a sting in his thigh. He was hit. Bosco's body smashed to the ground on the far side of the wall like a sack of potatoes and began to roll down the slight hill toward the road. More numb than in pain, Bosco got to his feet and began to carry on down the street, dragging his now useless leg behind him. Halfway down Cunningham Street, Bosco took a right. He was now into the maze of back-street lanes that were like a second home to him. Blood was streaming from his right leg and trailing along the street, but here in the alleys of the Jarro, Bosco knew he would be safe.

Back on Bosco's street, the army truck pulled away, loaded with soldiers, and leaving Bosco's father lying in the middle of the street. There was no point in arresting the old one-legged man now. He was dead.

The siren above the iron foundry was screaming, and a gush of steam was spouting from its whistle. Day's end. Constance turned the big key that locked the door bearing the legend "Accounts Office." She checked the handle and, satisfied it was secure, she began to make her way across the cobbled yard. Along her way to the exit, numerous members of her father's staff tipped their caps and wished her "Good night, miss." She returned the greeting, using the first name of each and every person, without smiling. It was not from any sense of aloofness that Constance did not smile; rather, it was a sense of self-consciousness. Her teeth. Constance was an attractive woman, to a point: dark-red hair and pale skin with green eyes. She could turn a man's head all right, so long as she did not smile. If God's blessing on Constance was that she be born to a comfortable home, then his curse was that he had given her the most ludicrous collection of teeth imaginable. They grew in every direction except straight and were quite large. When Constance Parker-Willis smiled it was like looking at a badly kept graveyard. So, happy or not, Constance smiled as little as possible. She left her father's foundry by the small gate on the western side, into Frowns Street. She buttoned up her coat, tied her headscarf, and pulled on her gloves. There was an icy chill in the air, and her breath was steamy in the early evening. She stuffed her hands into her pockets and began to make her way toward the City Centre, where she would catch the number-six tram home to Kingstown. She saw the body immediately as she turned into Windmill Lane. At first, from a distance, she thought he was a wino, lying drunk against the lamppost. The closer she got, the more apparent it became that this was a young boy. A dead or very badly injured young boy, for the pool in which he sat was blood, and not urine, as she had first thought. He was half propped up, and his chin was on his chest. She stooped over the boy and looked about for assistance. The street was empty. Constance knelt beside the boy and lifted his head. The handsome face of the boy took her breath away for a moment.

"Boy, wake up, boy." She spoke gently as she drew the raven-black hair from his face. She took off one glove and felt his neck for a pulse. It was there, but only just. She saw the rip in the right leg of the boy's pants and could see that this was where the blood was coming from. Laying the boy down, she tore open the pants leg, exposing the wound. Constance then removed her headscarf and made a tourniquet, pulling it tight around the leg. She now went back to trying to revive the boy.

"Boy, wake up, boy." She slapped his face. His eyelids began to move. "Come on, son, wake up." Slowly the boy began to come to. Constance heard men's voices at the end of the street. She drew a deep breath to call out.

"*Help,*" she screamed.

There were four of them, all workers from the foundry. They stopped in their tracks.

"You there," Constance cried out, "help me here."

"Miss Parker-Willis? Is that you, ma'am?" one of the men called.

"Yes, Thomas." She recognized him too. The men came toward her. She looked down at the boy. He was awake, his dark eyes were looking into her face. She was so relieved to see him show signs of life.

"It's all right, boy, help is here." She smiled at the boy. His lips began to move.

"What the fuck have you got in your mouth, missus?" the boy asked before passing out again. The men had now arrived. They immediately recognized the boy as "Hoppy" Reddin's son. They also knew a gunshot wound when they saw one; this boy needed a safe house.

Constance began ordering them: "You take his head. You there, cover him with your coat. I'll go for a doctor."

One of the men—Thomas, the man she had first recognized—held her arm. "Hold it, miss. We'll take him to a doctor, don't you worry about that," he said calmly.

"But he's been attacked. We should get the police," Constance insisted.

"You don't want to do that now, miss. You leave it to us." By now two of the men had lifted the boy and were walking away with him. Constance went to follow them. Again she was restrained by Thomas.

"Listen, miss, you done good. Probably saved the boy's life. Leave the rest to us. You go on home." Thomas smiled at her. He relaxed his grip and made after the other men, who were now rounding the corner at the top of the lane. Thomas turned.

"Miss. It would probably be best for everybody, including your good self, if you forget you ever seen this." He winked. In seconds Thomas was gone. Constance stood for a few moments, more than a bit confused. She never told anyone about that night, but she could not forget it. Ever.

CHAPTER THREE

The "safe house" the men had taken Bosco to was actually a two-room flat owned by Pascal Sheehy. Pascal had been a quartermaster in the old Irish Republican Brotherhood before they merged with Sinn Féin. Pascal had not been happy about the merger with Sinn Féin, but, a good solider, he had followed his leader, Michael Collins. Pascal had been enchanted by Collins since the big Cork man first arrived up in Dublin in 1916, and if Collins said it was good for the Brotherhood to merge with Sinn Féin, then he would follow. By the time Bosco had arrived in Pascal's flat, the young boy had lost a lot of blood and was very weak. His feverish temperature lasted for days, and Pascal spent many nights just dabbing the boy's forehead and upper body with a cool, damp cloth. Pascal did not know the boy at all, although he did have a passing knowledge of the boy's father, Sean "Hoppy" Reddin. He had never met Sean but had heard the many stories told about his wild exploits on behalf of the organization, as Collins' movement was known. Sean Reddin, Pascal had heard, after the 1896 Rising had escaped to Spain, where he spent some time fighting with some Spanish rebels. He had been injured, ironically, shot in the leg, in one of the skirmishes in the Catalan mountains. The injury had turned gangrenous, and Sean's leg had been removed. Over the following year, Sean had been nursed back to health by a young Spanish girl named Maria Augustino, whom he fell in love with. They went on to marry in 1904. The following year, Hoppy and Maria returned to Dublin. Two years later, shortly after the birth of their only child, Bosco, Maria died of consumption.

Pascal sat by the boy, staring into his face. The boy looked foreign all right. He had the look of a young Spanish bullfighter. The leg was healing and the boy would eventually return to full health. Pascal smiled and dabbed the boy's forehead with the cool cloth. He was happy in the knowledge that he had helped nurse him back to health and yet dreading the thought of when the boy was well again. For it would be Pascal that would have to tell Bosco he was now an orphan.

Constance's life at this time was particularly busy. The youngest of her three sisters, Joanne, was to be married. For Constance this meant that, as well as doing her job in her father's foundry, she would have lots of arranging to do at home. Even so, busy as she was, over the next few weeks her thoughts were constantly invaded by images of the young boy. She wondered: Where was he? Who was he? And was he still alive? She had asked around the foundry, but nobody seemed to know anything. Her inquiries were met with either blank stares or grunts of "I don't know what you're talking about, ma'am." Even from those men whom she had seen carry the boy away. So, eventually, she just stopped asking. With Joanne now becoming the third bride of the Parker-Willis household, Constance would be the only girl unmarried. Constance's mother, in an attempt, she was sure, to be sympathetic, would pat Constance on the hand and say things like, "For every old sock, there is an old shoe, dear." On the other hand, Constance's father would matter-of-factly bellow out his version of consolation: "Your Aunt Petunia died a spinster, and a very happy one at that. Marriage is not all it is cracked up to be, Constance dear."

Constance's mother would look dolefully at him and silently agree with a gentle "That's true." Of the two opinions, Constance couldn't decide which was worse. Her mother regarded her as an old sock, and her father, even though she was just twenty-five, was already talking in terms of her being a spinster. Constance tended to agree more with her father on the subject of marriage. Marriage maybe was not all it was cracked up to be. Certainly not the kind of marriages she saw her sisters and her mother live in. She had watched her sisters over the years, each one trying to be more beautiful than the others, constantly dressing up and appearing at social events looking like a gardener's exhibit. The sole purpose of which seemed to be to capture a man just like their father and then become invisible just like their mother. And Constance truly believed her mother had become invisible. For Constance had seen all the reasons a man would marry a woman vanish from her mother. Constance's mother had fulfilled her obligation of childbearing—and not too successfully, in her husband's opinion, for she had failed to produce a son. The children had been reared by nannies. All meals were prepared by the cook. The cleaning was done by the household staff. For conversation Constance's father went to the Men's Club on St. Stephen's Green, and his sexual appetite was satisfied by the many affairs he was having about the town. And so it was that Constance's mother was not required to provide her husband with food, intellectual stimulation, or sex. She was invisible. Constance Parker-Willis was not certain whether she were an old sock or indeed a spinster, but she was certain that she would *never* become invisible.

In any case, Joanne's wedding came and went. The wedding itself was identical to the two previous weddings of Constance's other sisters, and while Constance went back to work, over the next couple of months Joanne began her transition to invisibility.

• • • • •

Bosco sat on a hard kitchen chair by the open window, looking out
to the lane below. His leg was propped up on a wooden Guinness
crate. The wound had healed well, and although Bosco could walk
with a slight limp he found he tired easily. Spring had arrived, and
the sweet April air drifted in the window. He leaned forward out of
the window and looked down. Pascal was standing outside the door
of the flat, as he had been for the last thirty minutes. Waiting. At
the far end of the lane another young man stood in a tweed suit and
cloth cap. Just as Bosco looked toward the man, he turned and
whistled to Pascal. Pascal acknowledged his whistle with a wave
and promptly took the cigarette from between his lips. He threw
the butt on the ground and stood on it. He straightened his suit just
as a bicycle ridden by a very large man turned into the lane. Within
seconds the man on the bicycle was below the window. Bosco
watched as he casually swung his leg over the saddle and free-
wheeled the last few yards, to where Pascal stood. The man was
wearing a long brown gabardine coat and trilby hat. He exchanged
a few words with Pascal, and then the big man looked up at the
window, meeting Bosco's gaze. Pascal held the man's bicycle, and
Bosco could hear the downstairs door slam, then the heavy trudge
of feet coming up the stairs. The door of the flat opened, and the
man seemed not just to enter but to invade the room. His huge
form made the already small flat now seem tiny. The man made no
announcements or introductions. He took off his coat, held it over
his arm, took his hat off, and brushed back the fringe of hair that
dropped across his forehead.

"How's the leg, son?" His voice was deep and flat.

"Better," Bosco answered.

"Good," said the man. He now took one of the other kitchen

chairs and sat. From the inside pocket of his jacket the man took a brown manila envelope, and handed it to Bosco.

"You take the mail boat tonight, at eight o'clock. From Liverpool get the train to Crewe; change trains there for London. When you get to Euston Station you'll be met by a young man who will take you to your digs."

"What's his name?" Bosco asked.

"It doesn't matter," the man answered. He continued: "In this envelope is your mail-boat ticket and your train tickets, along with fifteen pounds in cash. Once you are safely in your digs you're on your own, son." The big fella went quiet and held Bosco's stare. Bosco turned away and looked out the window.

"Yeh, I know," Bosco said to the evening sky. There was silence for a few more moments. The big man stood. He dropped the envelope on the table and put his coat on. As he placed his hat on his head and adjusted it with the tips of his fingers, he gave a nervous cough.

"Your father was a good man, son," the man said and made for the door.

"My father's dead," Bosco answered.

"Aye, he is that," the man said with his back to Bosco. The man opened the door as if to exit but turned to Bosco. "Son," he called. Bosco turned and looked at the man.

"We all die sometime, son. When doesn't matter, how doesn't matter, all that matters is why." The big man winked and closed the door. Again Bosco could hear the heavy bang of the footsteps descending the stairs. The man arrived at the downstairs so quickly that Bosco thought he must have taken the steps two at a time. As he took the bicycle, no conversation passed between him and Pascal. The man simply took the bicycle, put his foot on the left-hand pedal, scooted along, cocked his leg over the saddle, and vanished around the corner. Bosco never saw Michael Collins again.

That night, Pascal left Bosco to the mail boat. There were no fond farewells, just a simple shake of hands.

"Thank you, Pascal," Bosco said.

"Good luck," said Pascal. He turned and was gone. At eight o'clock sharp, the boat pulled away from the North Wall Docks. There was a chill in the evening, but still Bosco stood on deck at the stern of the boat until the last of the lights of his native country disappeared below the horizon. It was a sad sight. The journey went exactly as Mr. Collins had dictated. At the train station in London, Bosco was met by a young man just a couple of years older than himself. He had walked up to Bosco.

"Reddin?" He simply said.

Bosco nodded. "Yes."

"Follow me." They walked the ten blocks to Bosco's digs without any further conversation.

Within days Bosco had found work on a building site as a laborer and, like many Irishmen before him, began building the country of his oppressors. Over the next eleven years, Bosco moved from building site to building site, traveling the length and breadth of the United Kingdom. He kept himself to himself and rarely indulged in the main weekend activities of those homesick Irishmen, which centered upon going to a local Irish pub and drinking until it didn't matter where you were. Instead Bosco drank in moderation. That is, except for one occasion.

That occasion was the day of August 23, 1922. Bosco had been working on a building site in Glasgow, just off Argyle Street. A tough job it was too, a bank, he was told. The building was to be constructed mainly of native blond stone. These were heavy blocks, and by the end of each day Bosco was more than usually exhausted. That evening, on his way back to his flat in the west end of Glasgow, Bosco stopped at O'Neill's Pub for a quick pint. O'Neill's was a very Irish pub, and it didn't matter what night of the week you went in, there was always a singsong going on or someone in the corner playing the fiddle or a rowdy game of darts. When Bosco was feeling down, he often made his way to O'Neill's just to cheer himself up a bit. This night, when he entered the pub it was crowded but totally silent. He walked slowly to the bar and ordered a pint of Guinness from what was, this night, a very lethargic barkeeper. There was no conversation in the pub, people just sat and sipped their drink. When the barman delivered the pint, Bosco took the first creamy sip from it and placed it back on the bar.

"What's up?" he asked the barman, nodding toward the silent crowd. The barman shook his head slowly.

"Th ... th ... they got the boss," the man replied with difficulty.

"What?" Bosco's brow furrowed.

The barman was now finding it very difficult to speak. "They shot him." He sobbed. "Michael Collins, they shot him, in Cork," the barman spluttered out, and then walked away shaking his head.

Bosco was drunk for three days solid. He was not alone. The length and breadth of England, Scotland, and Wales, Irishmen mourned in a drunken stupor.

During the following ten years the shock at the loss of Collins' life abated some in Bosco. He began to read more, and in the working-class city of Liverpool he found a new people's hero, union activist James Larkin. Bosco read everything and anything he could get his hands on, either written by or about Larkin. His anger was replaced by compassion and his sense of loss by a sense of purpose. Bosco Reddin grew up.

So it was that in 1932, when Bosco and Ireland were united again, the boy who left Dublin ten years previously returned a man.

CHAPTER FOUR

Dublin, 1932

When Bosco Reddin returned to Dublin, it was a very different place. The population were just getting used to independence, although partition had left its scar. He returned to his father's home to find it now occupied by his father's sister Julia. Aunt Julia welcomed him home with open arms, and he was soon settled in what was his old new home. Work in Dublin in general was hard to be found, although for a big, strapping young man like Bosco there were a few opportunities. There was some work in the Guinness Brewery. There were jobs going down on the docks. Bosco took neither, for Aunt Julia's husband, Dessie Regan, was working in the casting shed at the Parker-Willis Foundry and suggested to Cormac that he might try and find him a job there. Within three weeks of returning home, Bosco was working in a full-time job in the foundry.

When you begin a new job you don't get paid the first week; it's called a "back week." So Bosco didn't attend the accounts office for payment of his wages for two weeks. By then he was well settled in the place. His reputation had preceded him, and in some ways he was a bit of a hero in the area. Bosco had a quiet, friendly manner about him that had a calming influence on people and, although only two weeks working in the foundry, had already intervened in a couple of potentially dangerous fights. On the Friday of the second week, he lined up at the pay hatches in the accounts office with the others to collect his wages. There were five pay hatches, and he took the first one on the right. While he was queuing, the girl at the pay hatch in the center caught his eye. Unlike the other four pay mistresses, she was not in a uniform but wore day clothes. Also, Bosco noted, as she paid the wages to each man on her line she had a little friendly word for him. She addressed them all by their first names, and although she looked obviously a person of authority, the men seemed very comfortable with her. Bosco watched her until, eventually, he got to the top of his line. The young girl behind his hatch slid an envelope across and asked him to sign his name. Bosco smiled but ignored her request and opened the envelope, tossing the money out into his hand. He counted the cash and then pushed it back at the girl.

"This is short. Five shillings short," he said. Not antagonistic in any way. He just smiled. The girl was aghast; she was not used to being questioned.

"I beg your pardon," she said, but she didn't really.

"The wage packet here, love, it's a bit light, exactly five shillings light," Bosco repeated. Now, although this exchange was taking place very calmly and without any fuss, it still grabbed the notice of the men on the other lines, *and* the lady at the middle hatch, Constance Parker-Willis. Constance excused herself from the worker who was at the top of her line and went to the first hatch.

"Is there a problem here?" she asked, just as politely as Bosco had complained.

"No, miss, no problem, I'm sure it's just a mistake. Me wages is five shillings short." Bosco again was calm and smiled. Constance moved to the index box beside the girl and began flipping through cards until she came upon the name that matched the name on the wage packet—Bosco Reddin. She pulled out the card and began the perusal.

"Ah," she said, "here it is." She put the card down on the counter and turned it toward Bosco. "Now, you can see here that on Tuesday you didn't clock in until eight-fifteen instead of eight o'clock. Now, although that's only a quarter of an hour, if you are fifteen minutes late we stop one full hour's money," Constance explained.

"I wasn't late on Tuesday," Bosco simply stated.

"Yes, you were, look here where I'm pointing." Constance was getting a bit fussed now.

"I saw what you're pointing at, and I saw eight-fifteen. But I clocked in at eight o'clock, I always do, I'm never late. Your clock must be wrong; I can fix it if you like. I worked on clocks before," Bosco offered. Constance now became flabbergasted.

"But that's ridiculous. How could the clock just be wrong for you? I mean"—she waved at the man standing behind Bosco—"you there, Peter Bennett. What time did you clock in at on Tuesday?"

"A quarter to eight, ma'am. We all did, we always clock in at a quarter to eight on Tuesday," Peter answered, and dropped his eyes, for he feared embarrassing the lady, although around the room there were mumbles of "yes, we do," and nods of heads. Constance now began to rummage through the file box again and pulled out Peter Bennett's card. It did not read seven-forty-five; instead it read eight o'clock. Constance's mind was racing now. Every eye in the room was looking at her, and yet she could not just take these men's word for the fact that the clock was slow. She tried to be reasonable in her mind.

"Well, Mr. . . ." She glanced down at his name. ". . . Reddin. I will certainly have the clock checked, and if it is the case that the clock is in fact defective, I will make sure that you get your five shillings next week." Bosco smiled at her.

"I'll tell you what, miss, why don't you give me the five shillings and you get your clock checked and if it's not defective *I'll* give *you* back the five shillings next week." Constance stared at the young

man. He stood there smiling. Against her will she returned the
smile. She put her hand on the shoulder of the young girl standing
beside her.

"Catherine, go into my office and bring out five shillings, will
you?" she asked the girl. The girl scurried away.

"Thank you, ma'am," Bosco said, and touched his forelock. Bosco
left the factory that day with more than the five shillings. For, if his
reputation had preceded him and his actions over the previous two
weeks raised him in the workers' esteem, as he left the factory that
day with the five shillings, his reputation now was awesome.

The casting of iron is a dangerous business. For some reason that
scientists cannot explain, when you pour molten iron into water it
explodes. Thus it is vitally important that all casts are kept dry and
free of moisture. Horrific injuries and even death were commonplace in the Parker-Willis Foundry. However, they were no more
commonplace there than in any other foundry at this time. Every
man working there knew that injury and death came with the job.
Each time there was a death in the foundry, it affected Constance
deeply. Because she took such an interest in them, she knew most
of the workers by first name. She would ask them how their families
were, and keep herself abreast of the goings-on of most of the workers. Constance Parker-Willis attended the funeral of every worker
who died through accident or otherwise. Just weeks after her five-
shilling confrontation with Bosco Reddin, she was to meet him
again at one of these funerals. (In the interim period it turned out
that there *was* a tooth missing from the Tuesday cog within the
time clock. It was indeed skipping exactly fifteen minutes every
Tuesday. The clock was now repaired, and the workers had an extra
fifteen minutes' sleep on Tuesday mornings.)

The funeral itself had been a sad affair. The deceased was young

Liam Casey, just sixteen years of age. Liam's father, Pat, who had brought the boy to the foundry for work, was beside himself with grief. After the boy was laid to rest and the prayers were said, the gathering retired to the Gravediggers Pub, beside the graveyard. Constance paid her respects to the father and mother of the boy and then stayed to have a sherry, just to be polite. Suddenly there was a banging on the bar counter, and the entire room went quiet. Bosco Reddin stood up on a chair. As he did so, Constance Parker-Willis slowly sat down on one. When Bosco spoke, his voice was like music. And it commanded the ear of every person in the room.

"It was a sad thing we did today," he began. This was met by nods all around and pats on the shoulder for the boy's father. Bosco went on:

"It will be an even sadder thing if we allow it to happen so easily tomorrow."

From the middle of the crowd a voice bellowed, "There's nothing you can do about it, accidents will happen."

"Some accidents will, yes," Bosco bellowed out, "but some are not just accidents. Working a sixteen-year-old boy twelve hours a day is not an accident. Not having the proper clothing to protect yourself is not an accident. Walking the foundry floor in shoes that wouldn't keep the rain out, never mind molten iron, is not an accident." Bosco reached into the pocket of his jacket and pulled out a bundle of white papers; he held them in the air.

"See this? This is what Jim Larkin brought back from America. The Charter of Workers' Rights. Think about that now—workers' rights."

Another voice came from the crowd: "Larkin was a madman." There were a few grumbles among the crowd.

Bosco smiled. "Was he? Was he mad? Was he mad to want a worker to have more than the right to barely feed his family? Was he mad to want the worker to have paid rest days? Was he mad to want *you*, the workers, to go about your business, with your head held high, a sense of dignity about what you do, and a sense of pride in knowing that you were making the workplace a better place and a safer place for you, your own children?" He looked to Pat Casey. Casey nodded. Bosco carried on.

"This Charter of Rights was not written by Larkin, it was written by American workers. People just like you. It talks about safety, looking after the health of the worker, protection from unemployment, proper training and education, giving the hardworking man the dignity he deserves." Bosco pushed the papers back into his pocket. He took a deep breath, and his shoulders sagged. When he continued his tone had calmed.

"The Constitution of the United States of America opens with the words 'We the people'; the Proclamation of Independent Ireland started with 'people of Ireland.' They are just like us, and we are just like them, and if they can do it, we can do it. I urge you now, all of you . . . join the Irish Transport and General Workers' Union and unite with other workers who are trying to help make the workplace a better place for everybody, including the employers. Thank you for listening." Bosco stood down from the chair. There was slight applause but not much. Surprisingly, one of those applauding was Constance Parker-Willis. She was totally captivated by the young man. Someday, she thought, I would like to sit and chat with him.

CHAPTER FIVE

I t was a huge surprise to all. The announcement was made on a bright Sunday afternoon in the glass-paneled sunroom that overlooked the rear garden of the Parker-Willis home. The gardens themselves were beautiful and rivaled any garden in the area. Constance was sitting in one of the four huge wicker chairs that surrounded the African ebony table in the sunroom. Her legs were tucked beneath her, and an open copy of Charles Dickens' short stories lay on her lap. Constance's mother, sitting across from her, was concentrating on some needlework. As it was the game season, lunch had consisted of marinated pheasant, roasted and served in a peeled-grape sauce. Tasty but heavy, and Constance had intended to sit in the glass room and relax while the meal settled. She tried to relax but could not, tried to read but could not. Her concentration seemed to be all over the place, and she found herself reading the same paragraph over and over. Her mind seemed determined to wander in the quiet of the warm afternoon. Her father, Geoffrey, invaded the silence and the room.

"Excellent lunch, eh? I knew the moment I bagged that cock he would be delicious." He laughed loudly. He was of course referring to the bird he had just devoured. During the game season Geoffrey liked to go hunting quite a lot. The truth, of course, was that these hunts were mostly an excuse for him to get out of the house and meet up with his latest tart. On the rare occasion that Geoffrey did actually join in the hunt drive, he would become so drunk that he couldn't hit a bull's arse with a banjo.

"Yes, dear," Constance's mother gave her standard reply to all Geoffrey's statements.

"Gin and It, dear?" He asked his wife a rhetorical question, for as he asked it he was standing over her with the drink already prepared.

"Yes, dear." Constance's mother took the glass from her husband and placed it on a glass incidental table beside her. In studious mood, Constance watched all of this. Gin and It. This was the latest fashionable drink. The drink of the moment. The "It" referring to "IT"—"Indian tonic water." It seemed that the officers of Her Majesty's Forces in India found it difficult to take the required quinine on its own. So, instead, some bright spark had added a dash of tonic water and a dash of gin, to make it easier to swallow. Thus gin and quinine tonic was now the "in" drink. Constance thought about the gin now, her mind wandering again. Gin, she recalled, was once the drink only of prostitutes and mendicants, its consumption only seen in the brothels of London and bigger towns. In fact, "gin house" was a common term for a brothel. And yet here it was now, the same drink, regarded as a drink of class, upper class. Things change.

"I'm getting married." The words echoed about the glass room. Constance lifted her head from her book and glanced quickly around the room in search of the speaker of those words. Her mother looked up, needle poised mid-air. Her father was standing in one of the windows, looking over one of the gardens, at the gardener Murty, who was trimming some rosebushes. It was a couple of seconds before Constance realized that the words had come from her own lips. Her father didn't even turn from the window.

"Indeed, dear. Someday, someday. For every old sock . . ." he began, but Constance cut him short.

"The autumn. I'm getting married in the autumn." Again her

brain was screaming out the words without her permission. Geoffrey turned from the window; his face was steely. Constance smiled at him demurely, and when her father spoke there was more than a hint of sarcasm.

"Hear that, Mother. Poppy here is getting married." He took a sip of his drink. "In the autumn."

"Yes, dear." Mother did not even blink. Geoffrey paced the room.

"And who, may one ask, is the lucky chap? Or will you wait and introduce us all at the wedding ceremony?" he asked, again sarcastically.

"Bosco Reddin; you don't know him." Constance said, again following an argument between her brain and her lips. But Constance was wrong: her father did know him—well, at least he knew *of* him.

"The union activist?" he asked quietly. Then repeated the question at screaming pitch: "The *furking* union activist?" Even with the blood beginning to rise in Geoffrey's face, his pronunciation of "fucking" was old-school. The rage was becoming visible.

"Did you hear that, Mother? Your daughter thinks she is going to marry the union activist."

"Yes, dear," Mother answered, and did not take her eyes from her daughter's face. Now Geoffrey addressed himself directly to his daughter.

"Well, she can think again, Mother. Think again, I say!" Geoffrey downed the rest of his drink and began pouring another, his hands shaking with rage.

"I don't have to think again. I've made up my mind." Constance spoke with a firm voice. She was terrified but didn't show it. Now her father went into an absolute fury.

"Made up *your* mind? You don't have a mind in this house, missy! I make up *your* mind." He now struggled even to speak. He began to take deep breaths, an effort to calm himself. It didn't work.

"Why set your sights so high, dear? Why not the office boy, or that . . . shit shoveler out there?" He pointed out the window at Murty, the old gardener. Constance did not speak. She held her father's gaze. Her fear suddenly left her. She took in the sight of her father bent over, the veins throbbing across his forehead, his arm outstretched, pointing at the gardener.

"I think they may both be already married," she answered seriously. Her father spun and roared. He flung his drink across the room, the contents emptying over his wife. Both the window and the gin glass smashed when they met, the thick stump of the drinking glass being all that made it through the garden window. Bizarrely, Murty looked up, smiled, and waved.

With his entire body shaking spasmodically, Geoffrey now made to leave, and his parting words were calm, although his rage was very visible. He pointed and wagged his finger at Constance. "You. You do this, you do this, and you will leave this house with *nothing*. Do you hear me?" He screamed, *"Nothing,"* and he was gone. There was silence again except for the singing of the birds in the garden, which could now be heard through the broken window.

"Think about what you're doing," Constance's mother said softly. Constance looked at her mother sitting there. Her once-beautiful face, dripping in the gin that had spilled from her husband's glass. Constance stood and wiped her mother's face.

"I have, Mother. I have," she said softly. Constance's inner voice was speaking to her again: *You may have thought about it, but someone should tell Bosco Reddin about it.*

CHAPTER SIX

osco slid his clock-in card from the slot that next Monday morning. His eyebrows rose. His card had a note pinned to it. The note was folded and marked "private." Bosco looked about him, clocked in his card as normal, and, without reading the note, put it into his pocket. He replaced his card and made his way across the yard toward the casting shed. Halfway across the yard, he removed the note and unfolded it. It read, "Please call to see Miss Parker-Willis in Accounts at your earliest convenience, today." It was unsigned. He looked up to the windows of the accounts office.

"What's this about?" he said aloud. He decided to make his way to the casting shed first and let his supervisor know that he was here, before finding out the answer to his question. From two different upstairs windows his every action was being watched. Constance was watching. She was half hiding and peeking out her window, being most nervous as she had seen him unfold her note. As if she had written the whole story on that piece of paper. At another window Geoffrey Parker-Willis was watching. No hiding and peeking for him. He stood filling the window frame, his hands dug deeply in his pockets, his eyes fixed on Bosco.

When Bosco arrived at the casting shed, he waved to his supervisor. The supervisor came over. Bosco began to tell the man of his errand.

"I'll be back in a minute. I have to go to the office," Bosco roared over the noise of the machine and pointed at the office building.

"I know," the supervisor roared back. He pulled a rag from his pocket and wiped his perspiring brow with it. "What's that about?" he asked.

Bosco shrugged his shoulders and waved the note. "I don't know, but if it's Accounts it must be about wages?"

"Accounts?" The supervisor frowned.

"Yeh, Accounts," Bosco roared. He again opened the note and read it. "Yeh, that's right, Accounts," he confirmed.

The supervisor was shaking his head. "No. I was told to send you up to *his* office the moment you arrived. *His* office, not Accounts," the supervisor roared and pointed to the sky, as if the boss was indeed some kind of deity. Bosco was puzzled. He left the shed.

Constance watched Bosco re-enter the yard. She called out to her assistant. "Mary."

The girl stuck her head in the doorway. "Yes, Miss Constance?"

"Bring me some tea. Two cups, please." Constance smiled.

"Yes, miss." And the girl was gone.

Constance returned to the window to follow Bosco's progress, but he was no longer there. She scanned the yard quickly, and when she finally spotted him she paled. Instead of coming to see her, Bosco was now making his way up the steel stairs that led to her father's office.

"No," she cried, "no," and she banged on the window. But Bosco closed the door to the office, and she could see him no more.

Bosco didn't know what he had really expected. A secretary maybe, to ask him whom he wished to see? Or some suited people, scurrying from room to room, carrying piles of papers. Bosco had never been in any offices before, so his expectations were based on what he imagined they would be like. Whatever. He certainly didn't expect this. Nothing. He was standing in a kind of reception area alone. There was no sound of typing machines. Nor voices from behind doors. Nothing. He did notice that he couldn't hear any noise from the foundry itself. It was quiet. He wondered how they did that. Bosco was looking around the room and taking in the luxury of it all when he heard the rattle of a brass doorknob. It was the knob on one of the big mahogany doors. The big mahogany door opened and a man stepped into Bosco's area. The man was tall, high cheekbones. He wore his greased hair slicked back and sported a perfectly shaped and waxed mustache. He wore a tweed jacket into which he had just half his hand stuck with the thumb outside. Bosco didn't know who this man was, but he felt an instant dislike of the man and he could see it was mutual.

"Mr. Reddin?" the mustached man asked. His voice was crisp.

"That's me," Bosco advised.

"Do you know who I am?" The man wore a wry grin.

"No. But I'll bet you're not the janitor." Bosco winked.

"Ah, Dublin humor, where would you get it, eh?"

"Dublin?" Bosco offered as an answer.

"That was a rhetorical question, Mr. Reddin."

"And that was more Dublin humor, Mr. . . . ?" Bosco now knew the man's name, but he wanted the man to introduce himself.

"Parker-Willis. I am Mr. Parker-Willis," Geoffrey announced. Bosco took a casual look about the luxurious walnut-paneled offices.

"Of course you are." He smiled.

"Come into my office, Mr. Reddin," Geoffrey ordered as he turned his back and walked in ahead of Bosco. Bosco entered the lavish office and walked to and sat in the leather chair. Geoffrey turned, a little surprised to see the man seated without invitation.

Geoffrey spotted the door to the office still ajar. He pointed to the door.

"The door, Mr. Reddin." Bosco looked over at the door and feigned a puzzled look. Then Bosco pointed to a painting on the wall.

"The painting, Mr. Parker-Willis. You'll have to forgive me; I don't know how to play this game," Bosco apologized.

"I meant, shut the door, Mr. Reddin." Geoffrey spoke through his teeth.

"Oh, sorry, Mr. Parker-Willis. I work in the casting shed, I don't do doors. What you need is a doorman." Bosco smiled. Geoffrey returned the smile and crossed the room. He closed the door himself.

"I think we both know why you're here, Mr. Reddin," Geoffrey said as he made his way to the chair. He sat.

"I know why you're here, Mr. Parker-Willis. I have no idea why I'm here," Bosco answered, quite honestly.

"Oh, come, now, Mr. Reddin! You're hardly expecting me to just accept something like this? What did you think? That I would give you a big hug and start calling you 'son'?" Parker-Willis chuckled.

"Not without a fuckin' fight, Mr. Parker-Willis. You won't hug me without a fight." Bosco had no idea where this was going.

"My daughter is very important to me," Geoffrey started, and waited. Bosco thought there would be more to this sentence. He didn't realize he was expected to reply.

"Eh . . . that's nice," he managed.

"The thought of her marrying you may be very romantic to Constance, but you and I know the reality of it all would be . . . a disaster!"

Bosco's mouth hung open for some moments. He stared across the desk at Geoffrey as his mind took in the details of the last statement. Geoffrey, mistaking this for the shock of discovery and not for the shock of disbelief that it actually was, carried on.

"Yes. She told me. I know all about it." Geoffrey produced a cigar and lit it. Bosco quickly rooted in his pocket and pulled out a wrinkled half-smoked Afton cigarette. When they were both lit, Bosco spoke.

"She told you?" Bosco asked. Parker-Willis nodded knowingly.

"Now, look, Mr. Reddin, I have been around the course before. I know what you are up to, and I am a man who doesn't beat about the bush with these things." Geoffrey sat up and took a slow drag from his Havana.

"You know what I'm up to?" Bosco asked. Geoffrey nodded. "I see. So tell me, what am I up to, Mr. Parker-Willis?" Bosco was coming back from his shock now.

"Money." Geoffrey answered. Bosco's eyebrows lifted.

"Yeh think?" he said.

"Oh yes, Mr. Reddin. Money. It's always about money. She may think you love *her*, but it's money you love!" He chuckled and went on: "Constance is a fine girl, but she must be, what, I'd say ten years your senior? And she's not exactly a blossoming beauty, eh? So— come on, how much?" Geoffrey was in businesss mode now and felt very comfortable. He sat back and waited for the man's price. Bosco stood and walked to the window. He looked down at the filthy yard. He took a drag from his Afton and stared at the four huge chimney stacks spewing out the thick black soot-laden smoke that usually made its way into the Jarro. He turned.

"Make me an offer, Mr. Parker-Willis," he said. Geoffrey smiled and touched the fingers of both his hands together in a little arch.

"One thousand pounds, Mr. Reddin." Geoffrey spoke the mighty figure slowly, to give it impact. Bosco whistled.

"A thousand pounds would buy and furnish a good house, or buy and stock a shop, if a man had a mind to be a shopkeeper," Bosco said.

Geoffrey had a grin as wide as Dublin Bay. "Yes, Mr. Reddin, a lot of money. So what do you say?"

Bosco squashed his cigarette in the ashtray and ran his hand through his black mane of hair.

"Let me just talk to someone and I'll give you your answer then. Would that be all right, Mr. Parker-Willis?" Bosco asked.

Geoffrey stood and ushered Bosco to the door. "Of course, of course. I understand, Mr. Reddin. Let me know tomorrow." Geoffrey was all smiles now. He knew he had him, the man didn't even bargain.

"Oh, it won't take that long, Mr. Parker-Willis, just a moment," Bosco assured the man.

"Whatever." Geoffrey raised his hands. "Whatever." He charmed as Bosco left.

When he was gone, Geoffrey stood at his window over the yard and watched Bosco descend the steps. He saw him walk to the center of the yard and watched Bosco put a hand to each side of his mouth and begin to bellow. Bosco waited a moment and bellowed again. Geoffrey couldn't make out what the man was saying, so he opened the window and leaned out to hear.

Constance had cried at first, then stopped. Then she ran to the window, looked out, and cried again. Then she ran back to her chair and cried again. It had been fifteen minutes since Bosco disappeared into her father's office. Suddenly she saw the door to her father's office open, and Bosco began to descend the steps. She watched as he walked to the center of the yard. He looked up at her window and shouted: "Miss! Miss Parker-Willis."

She gave an involuntary yelp at hearing her name and ducked down, but she could still hear him.

"Miss Parker-Willis," he called again. The yelling was attracting attention now, and the workers appeared from out of every place.

"Miss Parker-Willis," Bosco called again. Bosco turned to the assembling crowd now. "What's her first name?" he asked them. They all shrugged their shoulders.

"Constance," came a voice from across the yard. It was one of the girls who worked in the wages office. "Her name is Constance," the girl repeated. Bosco changed tack.

"Constance," he called. "Constance Parker-Willis." Constance slowly rose and peeked over the windowsill. The yard was packed now. All eyes looking to her window. She could see her father too, he was standing at his window, leaning out to hear.

Bosco called again: "Constance, are you there?"

Constance stood, brushed herself down, wiped her eyes, and patted down her skirt. She took a deep breath and threw open the windows. She looked down on Bosco. There was a circle of people around him. Silence descended at her appearance. They looked at each other, she and he.

"Yes, I'm here," she called. There was a tremor in her voice. Bosco stepped closer to her window. "What do you want, Mr. Reddin?" she called. Bosco spoke loud enough for everybody to hear.

"Do you want to marry me?" he called up. All heads swung to look at Geoffrey Parker-Willis, then swung back to Constance. She was blushing so much her face glowed red. She stared at him. His face betrayed nothing of what he might be thinking. The words "Certainly not, you stupid man," sprung to her mind. She opened her mouth.

"Yes," she said. And her eyes began to fill. She felt as though she had ripped open her dress and exposed herself.

"Are you sure?" Bosco called out.

"Yes. I am sure, Mr. Reddin," she answered. There was no going back now. A tear dropped onto her wrist. There was silence in the yard. Bosco first, and then everybody else, turned toward Geoffrey Parker-Willis.

"Mr. Parker-Willis, stick your money up your arse. I'm getting married." The cheer in the yard was deafening. Geoffrey slammed his window closed. Bosco turned back to his new fiancée, a broad smile on his face. He smiled at her and winked. So much for the sitting with him and having a "chat," then.

CHAPTER SEVEN

Forty-one steps. Constance had counted each and every one of them as she climbed to the top of the tenement building. The building was an old Georgian structure divided into four "homes" of three rooms each. There was no bath in the building and just one toilet, which was on the second landing. The stairs were wooden from the second floor upward but granite from the hallway to the toilet. Each of the twelve rooms in the building had an open fireplace, which provided the only heating, and beneath the stairs on the ground floor was a shed divided into four storage units, each with its own padlock. This was where you stored your fuel, be it turf, slack, or coal. There was also room to store a few other things, if you had anything else to store.

Constance stood behind a breathless Bosco as he wrestled with the key in the lock of flat 4C. She heard the lock click loudly. Bosco turned the blackened brass knob and swung the brown wooden door open. He turned to her.

"It's not a palace," he said apologetically as he waved his arm wide for her to enter before him. Constance smiled nervously and entered what was to be her new home. She took in the center of the main room. It was gloomy. The room had one window to the world, and it was a multicolor of dirt and grime, from the green of algae on the outside to the brown staining of the coal and turf smoke on the inside.

"Switch on the light," she told Bosco over her shoulder without turning. He laughed.

"It is on," he said. She looked up to see a dull stained bulb doing its best to invade the gloom.

"Jesus," she mumbled under her breath. Through the dull light Constance surveyed her new home. The living room had a fireplace and four walls. In the corner off to Constance's right stood a four-ring gas cooker and oven. Beside this was a large Belfast sink precariously hanging on two brackets sticking from the wall. Over the sink was one brass pipe, which when Constance turned the faucet began to groan, bang, and then spurt ice-cold water. She looked at Bosco with a raised eyebrow.

"Needs a bit of work," he said.

Constance turned one of the brass fittings on the cooker. The *putt putt* and smell told her it was working. She moved to the window, undid the sash lock, and tried to raise the window open. It didn't move. From behind her Bosco mumbled. "Needs a bit of work too."

Constance wet her finger and ran it across the windowpane, leaving a clear streak on the glass.

"Who lived here before?" Constance asked.

"The Widow Clancy," Bosco answered.

"She could have at least cleaned the window," Constance moaned.

"She lived here on her own with five children, she hadn't time to look out the window, never mind clean it," Bosco answered with a disapproving edge to his voice.

"Sorry," Constance said. "I'm sorry. I didn't mean to . . ."

Bosco waved his hand before Constance could finish. "No, Connie, I'm sorry. I've been just waiting for you to complain. You're right, it wouldn't have taken much to clean the fuckin' window.

Look, as I said, it's not a palace." He held his arms out by his sides and tilted his head.

"No, it's not, and it probably never will be, but we can do our best to make it into a home," Constance said. They smiled at each other.

"The Penthouse." Bosco laughed. Constance joined in, gently at first, then loudly, then hysterically, until tears ran down her face. She put her arms around Bosco and they rocked back and forth, laughing with tears streaming down their faces.

Over the following six weeks, Constance would leave the iron foundry and go straight to 4C to work on the flat. Bosco would join her there when he was finished work, and they would work shoulder to shoulder to prepare their nest. Constance scrubbed and scraped, painted and polished. Bosco hammered and sawed and heaved and planed. Until, on October 11, 1933, just two weeks before they were to be married, Bosco and some of his friends carried the iron bedstead and mattress up the forty-one steps. They assembled the frame and placed it into the largest of the two bedrooms. With this done, the two surveyed their home. In the living room the wooden floors had been sanded and polished; over them was laid a square remnant of carpet that served as a rug. The ceiling, now with three coats of white paint, gleamed back the light from the 150-watt bulb Constance had acquired from the stores of the iron foundry. The walls were painted buttercup yellow and the dado rail white. The sink now had a cupboard built around it and a scullery cabinet beside it. The copper pipe and faucet were polished within an inch of their lives and gleamed gold over the sink.

CHAPTER EIGHT

The wedding bells clanged loudly across the parish for Bosco and Constance's wedding day. The bell-ringer, a young man named Michael O'Malley, was swinging from the bell rope with great enthusiasm. Like many of the young boys in the Jarro, Michael came from a republican family, and to him Bosco was a hero, a living legend. When he had rung out the call to sacrament, Michael hightailed it down to the vestry to dress for serving the Mass. Michael had become an altar boy at just four years of age. Now, at eight, Michael, although younger than most of the boys, was in charge of the altar boys in St. Jarlath's. This was one wedding he wanted to serve at the altar for himself. This was the importance attached to the wedding by the locals who knew and adored Bosco Reddin.

It was the most one-sided wedding ever held in St. Jarlath's Church. On the groom's side there was not a seat to be had. On the bride's side sat just four people. Three of them were waiting for confession, and the other was a wino the locals named "Pope" Charlie. He spent his time in churches drunk and shouting abuse at whatever priest was celebrating Mass. Bosco stood waiting at the altar in a suit borrowed from his uncle, a shirt borrowed from a friend, and new shoes he had bought himself.

Constance Parker-Willis knew that on the day she married Bosco, she would be thrown out of her father's home. She was to receive no dowry, no allowance, and was to be released from her father's will. She left her home with just the clothes on her back, with the exception of one gift. Just before she had departed, Constance's mother came to her room. She handed Constance a large box.

"Take this," she said to her daughter. "It is all I own, and I want you to have it." Constance took the box. She hugged her mother and kissed her on the cheek.

"Thank you, Mother. I'm sorry," Constance managed to get out through her sobs.

"Don't be sorry, dear, be happy," her mother said. And added, "I wish it were me." With her head bowed, she left the room.

When Constance arrived at the church, she was wearing the contents of the box her mother had given her. The veil that sat beneath the glittering tiara was a white mesh of silk. The bodice of the wedding gown was covered in a thousand pearls, all hand-sewn, and the flowing skirt was made up of white satin covered by a second skirt of handwoven Galway lace. Without doubt it was the most beautiful wedding dress to have graced the aisle of this church. And its crowning glory was the sixteen-foot silk-and-satin train that gently glided behind the bride as she made her way up the aisle. At the altar Bosco stretched out his arm and took her hand. Believe it or not, this was the first time Bosco Reddin had ever touched his bride, and his smile betrayed how beautiful and soft her skin felt.

The ceremony itself was uneventful—well, up to the taking of the vows anyway. For it was at this point that Pope Charlie woke up in his pew and joined in the proceedings. When the priest asked Bosco, "Do you take this woman to be your lawfully wedded wife?," Pope Charlie got in first with, "Of course he does, he fuckin' turned up, didn't he."

"I do," said Bosco.

"And do you take this man . . ."

"Same question, same fuckin' answer." Charlie was bored.

"I do," Constance said, looking into her husband's dark eyes.

At the end of the ceremony it was time for the bride and groom to make their way into the vestry to sign the Registry Book. The priest would lead the way, followed by the witnesses, then Michael O'Malley, finally the bride and groom. Just inside the door to the vestry, Bosco halted. Constance went on a little before she realized that she was walking alone. She turned.

"Are you all right, Bosco?" she asked.

"Yeh, I'm fine. Come here for a moment. Before we go in there."

"Why? What's wrong?" Connie had a worried look.

"Is everything all right, Bosco?" It was Michael O'Malley. Over Connie's shoulder Bosco waved him on.

"Fine, son, fine. Go ahead of us and tell the priest we'll be with him in a minute." Michael gave a thumbs-up sign.

"No bother, Bosco." And he was gone. Constance made to speak, but Bosco put his finger to her lips.

"Shush." He smiled. "Hush for a minute and listen to me." Connie nodded her head. His eyes were locked on hers as they stood huddled together in the corner of the hallway. When Bosco spoke, it was just above a whisper. "I know this has all happened very fast. And I know that we have stood out there and made promises and recited our lines. But there is something I want to say to you. Not out there, in front of all of them. Just me to you, but I want to say it here in the house of God. Constance Parker-Willis, I love you." He waited a moment. "Do you believe that?" Constance's eyes began to fill. For she realized that no man had ever spoken those words to her before. Not even her father. Now here she was, penniless, just the clothes on her back, disinherited, and up to recently homeless. And for the first time she felt truly loved. As the warm, glistening tears sprang forth, she nodded her head to her new husband and whispered, "Yes. I believe that."

Bosco smiled. He cupped his hand beneath her chin and lifted her face to his. Gently he kissed her on the lips. "I will never leave you, Connie, and wherever you go, woman, walk gently, for you carry the heart of this man with you."

Constance smiled. "I will walk as if I am on feathers," she promised.

Now he smiled. "Good. Now, there's just one more thing." He fished in his pocket and produced a headscarf. It was folded, and he placed it in her hand. She looked down at the scarf.

"What's this?" she asked

"It's yours," Bosco replied. Constance was still puzzled.

"Where did it come from?" she asked.

"It came from around my leg, a long time ago." A dawning crossed Constance's face.

"You were the boy . . ." she stammered out.

"Aye. And you are the angel. Come, let's make it official." The rest was a blur to Constance.

At one point during the signing of the registry the priest leaned over to Constance and whispered, "I'm so sorry about the shouting during the ceremony."

"What shouting?" Constance asked, and she meant it.

The wedding breakfast that followed was attended by over a hundred guests, including Pope Charlie, and was the usual bawdy affair, with just one note that should be mentioned. In his speech Bosco referred at all times to his new wife as "Connie," and he would do so from that day onward. She would never hear the name Constance again. A new name, a new beginning, and a whole new world.

CHAPTER NINE

Over the first twelve months of their marriage, Bosco encouraged Connie to make an effort to reconcile her differences with her father. He knew well the dreadfully lonely feeling of being an orphan and would have given anything to have just one more day with his father. She did, but to no avail. She went to work every day, and not only did she have no words with her father, she never even clapped eyes on him. Her sisters had disowned her, and her mother was held incommunicado. Then, when Connie became pregnant, she retired from her job at the foundry, so the chances of reconciliation were further reduced.

On the sixth of December, 1934, Connie gave birth to a beautiful baby girl. She weighed in at six pounds and seven ounces. She had a mop of raven-black hair and screeched nonstop through her first ceremony when, four days later, she was brought to St. Jarlath's and baptized Agnes Loretta Reddin, after the Blessed Agnes. The birth of Agnes prompted the last ever attempt to rejoin Connie with her family. With babe in arms, Connie boarded the tram and made her way to her former home in Kingstown. The house had not changed, but seemed bigger than she had remembered. She pulled the door chain. The door was opened by a maid. A new one. She was a good-looking young girl.

"Yes? Can I help you?" she asked.

"Could you tell Mr. Parker-Willis that Constance is here?" Connie smiled at the girl. She didn't return it.

"What's wrong with you, woman! Did you not see the sign on the gate? No beggars!" the maid scolded.

Constance held her temper. "I am his daughter, Constance Parker-Willis, and this is his granddaughter, Agnes. Now, if you cannot get my father, then send Mr. Pratchett out here." Naming the butler had the desired effect, although the girl still made Connie wait at the door while she checked things out.

When the girl returned some minutes later, she was perplexed. "Mr. Parker-Willis says he does not wish to see you today or any other day. And he told me to give you this for your child." The girl stretched out her hand, in which she held a single pound note. Constance stared at the money for a moment. She did not take it.

"Thank you," is all she said as she walked away from her family for the final time. Her babe in arms, she returned home to the Jarro. Connie never told Bosco the sorry tale.

Little Agnes Reddin had been a beautiful baby from the moment she was born. Her mop of soft, dark hair and beautiful tan-brown skin drew the attention of every Dubliner that passed the child's pram. She grew up those first couple of years believing that adults only said "Oooh!" and "Aah!" As Agnes was a small-born baby, her mother, Connie, had been maybe a little overly protective in the child's early years. Maybe.

In any case, the baby Agnes grew rapidly into a bonny child, and blossomed with even more beauty as she approached her school-going years. She was a quiet child. Too quiet sometimes. Connie worried that if she should remain this quiet she would lack confidence when she got older. She mentioned this to the nun on Agnes' first school day.

"A quiet girl, is she? Quiet is good, Mrs. Reddin. What would you prefer? A screaming brat like most of the little tramps in here?" the sister yelped at her. Connie was even more nervous now, leaving her pride and joy with this awful woman.

Agnes' first few years in school passed without note. She remained a quiet girl over the first four years and was barely noticed, keeping to herself. However, when she entered Holy Communion class, this was about to change. Connie need never have to worry again about her daughter's "confidence." Agnes was about to meet Marion Delany.

Thanks to that first day's encounter with Marion, Agnes now looked forward to each day in school. And even Marion was now attending school most days, and sometimes stayed even for the whole day. It was a wonderful time for both of them. But when they would look back on this time years later, the one thing they would remember most of all was the day they both went to the church for their very first confession. Agnes' befriending Marion Delany was to be a huge milestone in her life, and in that same year, yet another milestone was to arrive. Or should that be millstone?

CHAPTER TEN

Agnes was nearly five years old that day when her mother disappeared for the first time. Agnes had arrived home from school at three-fifteen. She had had a wonderful day at school. She had learned nothing at all, but Marion had stayed in school for the whole day, and they whispered to each other and giggled every time the nun's back was turned. When Agnes walked the short couple of blocks and arrived home to her building, she was so happy that she bounded up the steps to her flat. The front door was closed, as usual, but today when she knocked there was no answer.

She tried calling through the gap at the bottom of the door. With her face pressed against the floor she called: "Mammy? Mammy, it's me, open the door." This is fun, she thought. She changed her voice to a monster's voice, speaking each word slowly: "Ooo . . . pen . . . daa . . . doooor." And then she giggled. She did this for about fifteen minutes. Now she was bored, so she lay on her back with her feet up against the door and began banging on the door with her feet. She pretended she was walking up the door—*bang, bang, bang.*

A voice shouted from another landing somewhere in the building: "Stop that fuckin' banging!" The voice screeched.

"My mammy won't open the door," Agnes called back.

"Then get yourself adopted, but stop the fuckin' banging." She heard a door slam.

Agnes sat on the floor, resting her back against the door. She began to cry, very quietly lest the voice from the other place in the building call out again. As she sat there and wept, all kinds of horrible things went through her mind. What if her mammy had gotten lost? Who would come here and open the door? Maybe her mammy and daddy had gone away and forgotten all about her? Sobbing softly, she fell asleep. When she awoke, it was now dark and she was so cold she was shivering. She had never been on this side of the door when it was dark, Mammy wouldn't allow her. Agnes started to become very frightened. Suddenly there was a bang from the downstairs street door, and she heard footsteps climbing up the stairs. She started to panic now. There were no more stairs up, so she could only go down! This was no good, the footsteps were coming up and getting closer. In the corner she spied a crumpled sack, so she went to the corner and covered herself with the sack. She was sobbing with fear, and in an effort to stop the sobbing she held her breath. It didn't work: the sobs just came out louder. The footsteps got louder, until she could tell they had reached her landing. Then they stopped. Just for a moment; now she could hear them again, coming toward her corner.

"Who's that in the corner?" the deep voice boomed. Agnes began to cry out loud. She was so scared she had not recognized her father's voice. Bosco lifted the sack from off his daughter and smiled when he saw her there, squashed up as small as she could get, crying with her eyes tightly shut.

"Agnes? Agnes love, what are you doing out here?" Bosco asked as he lifted the child into his arms. She opened her eyes and, on seeing her father, wrapped her arms around his head so tightly that he could not breathe. He had to peel her off his face.

"Oh, Daddy, Mammy won't let me in," she cried. Holding Agnes with one arm, Bosco moved to the door. He fished a key from his pocket. A quick twist and he pushed open the door. The flat was in darkness. Bosco flicked on the light switch.

"Connie?" he called. There was no answer. Still carrying Agnes, he looked into the two bedrooms. Both empty. Back in the main room he spotted a note on the table. He gently put Agnes down and read the note.

"Oh my God," he exclaimed as he read, and then dropped the note and began to run around the rooms, grabbing clothes and stuffing them into a bag. He opened his free arm and stooped low.

"Come," he said to Agnes. Bosco carried her down the stairs, and when they got outside he took her hand. Together they walked through the dark streets. When they arrived at Bosco's Auntie Florrie's place Agnes recognized it. Bosco banged on the door, and Conor, Florrie's husband, opened it. Bosco placed Agnes by the fire and went into the kitchen to talk to Florrie and Conor. When he came out again, he walked straight to Agnes and knelt down beside her.

"Agnes love, Auntie Florrie is going to mind you here tonight. I'll come and get you after school tomorrow." Agnes began to cry.

"It's all right, sweetheart," her father soothed her. He lifted her tiny chin. "And I'll tell you what. When I come and get you tomorrow? I just might just have a big surprise for you." He smiled. Agnes wiped her eyes. "Surprise?" she repeated every child's favorite word. Her father nodded and smiled. She kissed her daddy, and then he was gone. She was so hungry, but she didn't say anything to Auntie Florrie, it wouldn't be manners, so when she was put to bed her tummy was so empty it was paining her. She still had not gotten over her ordeal, and even as she slept the odd huge sob would stagger from her lips. Next morning, she came down the stairs to find Aunt Florrie all jolly in the kitchen. Agnes sat at the kitchen table and within minutes had devoured two bowls of porridge.

"My gosh," Florrie exclaimed, "you like your porridge, don't you?"

Actually, Agnes hated porridge, but she was so hungry that she would have eaten Uncle Conor had Auntie Florrie served him up.

As soon as Agnes arrived at school, she went in search of Marion to tell her of her ordeal. She looked everywhere but to no avail. Agnes prayed that Marion would not miss school today of all days. When the school bell sounded, all the children began to assemble into their lines. Agnes stood in her line looking around feverishly for any sign of Marion. The line began to move toward the school door, and Agnes saw Marion tearing across the schoolyard. She was late, but Agnes was just relieved that she was there. As soon as they got out to little break, Agnes took Marion aside and told her the whole story. Marion listened with great interest. By the time Agnes had finished telling the story, especially the piece about the surprise, Marion was grinning from ear to ear and nodding knowingly.

"It's a baby," announced Marion.

"What is?" Agnes asked.

"Your surprise. It's a baby. Your mammy's gone to get a baby." Agnes stood rooted to the spot, her mouth open wide, staring at Marion.

"But how do you know?" Agnes asked.

"Its always a baby. Every time your mammy goes away and your daddy says, 'We might have a big surprise tomorrow'"—she mimicked Agnes' father—"it's a baby. It always is. We've had so many surprises in our house that me mother can't feed them all. It's a baby, I ought to know." Marion of course came from a household that was so large that some of the children didn't even know the others' names. Agnes was shocked and stunned.

"But, but," she stammered, "my mammy and daddy already have a baby, *I'm* their baby."

"You're not a baby anymore, Aggie, you're a young wan."

The bell sounded for the end of the break. Marion trotted back into the class. Agnes dragged her feet slowly behind her. As promised, Agnes' father was indeed waiting outside the school gates when she finished school. She ran to him and threw her arms around him. He was all cleaned up, like it was Sunday, and he was beaming with joy.

"Come on, missy, let's get on home; I have that surprise for you." He smiled. He took her hand and they began to walk. Agnes stopped and looked up at her father. He looked down. "What?" he asked.

"My surprise, is it a baby?" she asked. Bosco's eyes widened and he began to laugh.

"How did you know? Yes, it is a baby! A beautiful little sister for my Agnes," he announced.

Agnes stomped her foot. "I don't want it. Give it back!"

Bosco took her by the hand, and they walked home in silence to meet Agnes' new sister.

Connie was sitting in the armchair, a tiny bundle in her arms. She was smiling. Agnes was not. Connie motioned Agnes to come closer with a wave of her hand and whispered, "Come, Agnes, come meet your new sister. Her name is Dolly." Slowly Agnes went over and tried to peek in at the bundle. She angled her head this way and that. Connie pulled the blanket down slightly, and Agnes could see this pink wrinkled "thing" chewing its hand.

"Isn't Dolly beautiful?" Connie asked.

"Maybe it'll die," Agnes said.

"Agnes, don't be so nasty," her mother admonished her.

"I hope it does die," Agnes said through pouting lips, and stomped off to her bedroom for a cry. Bosco stayed in the flat for just half an hour, then made his way back to the foundry to work. Connie went to the bedroom, and after she fed the baby, she and the baby had a nap. When Agnes came out of the bedroom, the flat was quiet. She turned on the radio and sat listening to the music. Agnes, even at five years old, was beginning to learn how to be alone.

Despite Agnes' first hope for the child, Dolly didn't die. Like many second-born children, Dolly was spoiled at every turn, leading Agnes to feel a little neglected, even though she was not. And worse was to come as she grew older, for on Dolly's first week in school, Connie insisted that during the breaks Agnes was to hold Dolly by the hand for the duration. She hated it, but she did it. At times so tightly that Dolly's hand lacked blood flow.

Dolly took to school well, and Agnes' life was diverted by her preparation for her first confession.

CHAPTER ELEVEN

"How do I look, Mammy?" Agnes asked. Connie studied her daughter carefully.

"Like a beauty queen," she proclaimed.

"Ah, no, really, Mammy. Do I look all right?" the little girl begged.

"Agnes dear, you will be giving your confession in the dark. The priest won't see you."

"God will. He sees everything, and He's everywhere," Agnes spouted her newfound knowledge.

"Well, then, if it's God you are trying to please, you look good enough." Connie was concentrating. She had marked the pattern of the dress out, using blue chalk. Everything was ready, but she was still trembling, the cutting shears felt heavy in her hands. It had been the same on the two previous occasions when she had had to cut into the train. For the christening robe for Agnes and then later Dolly. This satin train had been on the wedding dress, untouched, for three generations. She was not cutting it by choice, but her child needed a Communion dress and she was going to have one. Connie was about to close the blades of the shears.

"It's so beautiful, Mammy!" Agnes screeched with delight. Connie jumped with fright.

"Agnes dear, why don't you run along to school now. Like a good little girl." Connie put the shears down gently as she spoke.

"Okay. Bye," and Agnes was gone.

Connie decided to have a cup of tea and calm down before trying the cutting again.

The children were lined up into two lines. They were instructed to
hold hands with the person beside them. Then, like a wagon-train
boss of the old American West, Sister Benedict raised her hand and
the group began to move. The trek was on to St. Jarlath's Church
for the big day.

The forty-one little girls snaked their way along the footpaths,
the May sunshine on their faces and old dears "cooing" as they
passed. Soon they arrived at the gigantic front doors of the church,
and the smiles vanished from their faces. Now they slowed in their
walk, passing through the doors silently, each girl dipping her fingers in the font of holy water and making the sign of the cross. Sister Benedict ushered them to a pew beside one of the confessionals.
She halted them before they could enter. She had not figured out
her problem yet. Should she get Marion Delany to be the first to go
and get her out of the way, or should she hold her back to last, so
that any trouble she caused could be minimized by a swift exit? She
decided on the former.

"Delany," she whispered down the line, and motioned for Marion to come front and center. Marion arrived still holding Agnes'
hand. Without explanation she ushered the two girls down the
pew, and the rest followed.

The confessor for the big day was Father Angelus. An old cam-
paigner. He was already installed in his center cubicle, awaiting the
toddlers' invasion. These were straightforward. The child would
enter. The sins confessed were a narrow range, and most usually
got by with, "I disobeyed my father and my mother." He peeked
through the red velvet curtains and watched the children take their

places. Sister Benedict came to the curtain and whispered, "Ready, Father?"

"Ready, Sister. Let them go." He crossed himself and kissed his scapulars. Sister Benedict gave a nod to Marion and Agnes, and they entered the boxes on either side of the priest's cubicle. Marion knelt in the darkness and waited. Suddenly there was a wooden *thud* sound as the priest pulled back the window cover. A small shelf protruded from the bottom of this window for the sinner to lean his/her elbows on. With Marion now on her knees, the shelf was six inches above her head, and she could see nothing.

"In the name of the Father, the Son, and the Holy Spirit," the priest rattled off quickly, and to Marion this was just a voice in the darkness. This was Marion's cue to begin.

"Hello? Father, are you there? Hello," she whispered.

"What, what's that?" the priest said; he was squinting, trying to see if there was anyone there. "Stand up, child." Marion did, and the priest could now see her little eyes peeping over the shelf. Marion didn't know why she was told to stand, as all rehearsals had been done kneeling, so she awaited further instructions in silence. The priest now took this as the girl being stagestruck at her first confession, so he tried to help her. "Bless me, Father, for I have sinned," he hinted to her. Now Marion was completely confused: this was *her* line. She now thought someone else had skipped in front of her.

"Hey, mister, fuck off, I was here first." She was having none of it. She took a deep breath and went for it.

"BLESS ME, FATHER, FOR I HAVE SINNED," she said at the top of her voice.

"Aghhh!" Father Angelus yelped with fright.

"THIS IS MY FIRST CONFESSION," she went on.

Father Angelus was now pressed back against the wall in an effort to get away from this voice. "Who is this?" he called.

"I SLAPPED ME LITTLE BROTHER . . . TWO TIMES. I STOLE TWO PENNIES ON ME MOTHER . . ."

Father Angelus was now leaning out through the curtains looking for Sister Benedict, who had been lighting a candle to the Virgin Mary at the far side of the church but was now scrambling across pews to get to Marion.

"Sister, Sister," the priest was calling in minor panic.

"I'm coming, Father," the breathless nun called back.

The other children were giggling, and Agnes was in tears with laughter on the floor of the opposite cubicle. However, everything came to a sudden silence at Marion's finish. Which coincided with the nun's arrival.

"I ATE MEAT ON A FRIDAY . . . I DISOBEYED ME FATHER AND ME MOTHER . . . AND I LET JOHNNY HANNIGAN SEE ME KNICKERS."

The nun froze. The priest froze, and the children froze. Marion waited for her absolution. The silence prevailed. Everybody with his or her own thoughts. The little girls thinking of Johnny Hannigan. Needless to say, it was Marion that broke the silence.

"ARRAGH! WHAT'S THAT SMELL? DID YOU FART, FATHER? THAT'S NOT ME PENANCE, IS IT, FATHER?"

Father Angelus blushed, Sister Benedict went pale, the girls giggled as they watched Marion leave the cubicle with the help of Sister Benedict, faster than an ejector seat.

It was a day to remember. The Communions went beautifully. Agnes was the best dressed, in satin and silk made from her mother's wedding-dress train. But the star of the show was Marion Delany and the telling and retelling of her first confession.

CHAPTER TWELVE

L ife was getting a little better for Connie and Bosco too. The foundry was now fully unionized, and conditions had improved some for the men. Bosco had been elected onto the branch committee of the union, and he loved his involvement.

The insecurity felt by Agnes at having to share her parents' attention with Dolly was tempered somewhat by the excitement which Marion brought into her life. The following years, for Agnes and Marion, were the most fun-filled anyone could ever have. Marion would constantly regale Agnes with the funny stories that she would tell of a place she called "the Markets." It seemed to Agnes that "the Markets," whatever it was, was at the center of the universe, and that Marion and her family were the center of "the Markets." The place existed only in Agnes' mind and Marion's stories. Agnes pleaded with Connie every day to allow her to go with Marion to this place. Connie managed to hold out, just, until Agnes was twelve years old. When she said "yes" to Agnes that first time, her daughter gave her the biggest hug she had had in years. The night before her trip to "the Markets," Agnes barely slept she was so excited.

Of all of the endearing characteristics of the Markets, the one most notable and unique is the speed and frequency with which one can be insulted by a Moore Street dealer woman. Their tongues are as fast as lightning and can crack like a bullwhip. And with each lash they take a layer of skin off of the most hardened ego.

There are no double standards on "the street." The women apply citrus wit to each other just as much as to a passing customer. For instance, whereas in most pleasant circles a person's individualism, such as minor blemishes on one's beauty, would not be mentioned, not so in Moore Street. Fact is, if it were obvious enough, it would probably be added to your name! Thus you have people with names like Hopalong Hannah, who had been the victim of an accident some years ago that left her with a stiff leg. Or two of the fish sellers, Winnie the Mackerel and Smelly Nelly. The woman with the excessive body odor was Sweaty Betty. Across from her stall was a woman that had had so many surgical procedures on a congenital vaginal deformation she was addressed simply as Funny-Fanny. Believe it or not, these were regarded as names of affection.

Most of the "on-street banter" which was shouted from stall to stall across the street concerned sex. The lack of, or the size of, or the length of, or the shape of. Many visitors to Moore Street Market would just stand in one spot simply listening to the exchange of words, insults, and slagging matches, sometimes shocking in content but always funny.

Agnes Reddin had always thought of Moore Street as a place of mystery. Marion referred to it always as "the Markets," and her descriptions of it to Agnes always made it sound so beautiful, like it were somewhere on another planet. When Agnes arrived in Moore Street for that first time, she was not disappointed. Agnes walked behind Marion from stall to stall as Marion described each one and gave Agnes little tips. At the flowers, there were buckets of gardenias, gladioli, lilies, asters, and daffodils.

"You always put a couple of aspirins into the flower water. That keeps them fresh for longer." Marion spoke with the authority of an expert. Agnes just nodded, taking it all in. As they walked along the market street, Agnes was filled with excitement, while Marion was greeting every dealer by name. Most were related to her somewhere along the line anyway.

"How'ya, Lily," Marion said to the stall holder.

"How'ya, Marion love," the woman replied.

When they had moved on a little, Marion turned to Agnes. "That's *really* her name, Lily. It's not made up nor nothing. That was a good idea by her mother, wasn't it? Like if you have a flower stall call your baby Lily." They laughed.

"I have an uncle called Bismarck," Agnes said.

"Bismarck? Is that a flower?" Marion asked.

"I dunno." They moved along. Agnes also enjoyed the continuous banter, but understood little of it.

"Hey, Funny-Fanny," a dealer called across the street, holding up a huge, freshly dug carrot.

"What?" answered Funny-Fanny.

"This carrot reminds me of my old man's tool," she exclaimed

"What do yeh mean, the size of it?" Funny-Fanny asked.

"No, the dirt of it," the dealer called back, eliciting laughter from stallholders and customers alike.

Marion gave Agnes the guided tour as they tripped along down Moore Street toward the Henry Street end. The place was awash with color, scent, and stench. There were golden and scarlet apples, juicy pears, hairy peaches, bananas, oranges, white and red grapes, cherries, plums, strawberries, raspberries, gooseberries, and rhubarb. On the vegetable stalls there was cabbage, white cabbage, green cabbage, flat Dutch cabbage, red cabbage, Savoy cabbage, there were carrots, onions, mushrooms, turnips, parsnips, Pentland Dell potatoes, Queens, Pinks, Whites, leeks, asparagus, broccoli, spinach, sprouts, peas, and French beans. Over in their own little area, well away from the other stalls, stood the fish stalls. Mountains of ice across which lay fresh mackerel, sole, plaice, rainbow trout, eels, cod, salmon, cod roe, ray, whiting, halibut, whitebait, crab, lobster, and Dublin Bay prawns. Then you had the "mixed and dairy" stalls. These were the vendors of duck eggs, goose eggs, hen's eggs, and herbs and spices like nutmeg, ginger, parsley, cinnamon, mint, and thyme, or dried fruit, dates, and garlic. The street, so packed with chatter, scent, and melodious insults, became Agnes' second home. Yes indeed, it was a wonderful time for the two young wans.

CHAPTER THIRTEEN

Agnes had tried to keep her breasts a secret for as long as she could. She didn't like them, and they hurt. Puberty is a difficult time for any young girl, but when it comes early and you are the only girl in your class in school sporting a swollen chest and a whiff of pubescent hair it can be truly embarrassing. It was also confusing for Agnes, who did not fully understand the changes that were taking place in her body and, by extension, her life. Not that she and the other girls in Agnes' class in school had not had a modicum of sex education. They had. Well, all except Marion, who had been put out of the class after just ten minutes and three questions. The questions Marion had asked were just for clarification. When the sister had said "breasts," Marion asked if this was the same as "diddies," and then did "vulva" mean her "wiggie." These two were followed by her ejection question, which was, "Is 'penis' the same as 'cock'?" All the other girls were thinking these questions, but, as usual, only Marion would ask them. The sex-education class lasted one half-hour. This half-hour talk on that day in a language that, as Marion displayed, is alien to the girls was to be their total formal sex education. The warnings were there, of course, and the sister made the girls write them down:

(1) Never wear black patent shoes with a skirt, as boys could see the reflection of your knickers in them.

(2) Makeup is only used by harlots and prostitutes.
(3) Dancing closely so that your body touches against a boy's body would bring trouble. For, the sister explained, once boys were aroused they had no control of their actions, and anything that followed would be the girls' own fault.
(4) And, of course, all of the above were a one-way ticket to eternal damnation in hell.

The young girls left the class that day half informed and completely terrified.

It was that same day that Agnes was going to tell her best friend her secret. No better time than after sex class to reveal that you had begun to grow. But before she could, Marion began to tell another story that was to give Agnes another cause for hating her early start in the breasts department. The two had been walking home and discussing the lesson that day. Agnes had been shocked by hearing how babies were made. The thought of her parents doing anything like that was just upsetting. And the thought of Marion's parents doing it *so many times* was positively revolting. The conversation died for a while, and the girls walked side by side toward the tenements.

"I don't want any diddies," Marion suddenly said.

"What?" Agnes was aghast. "Every girl gets diddies."

"I hope I don't, or if I do, I hope they're real small ones, just this big." She held her fingers slightly apart.

"Why?" Agnes had not given any thought at that stage to shape or size.

"I don't want to end up like me Auntie Tessie."

"What's wrong with your Auntie Tessie's diddies?" Agnes asked.

"Well, I've seen photographs of her when she was just getting married, and her diddies were out to here." Marion held her hands as far away from her chest as she could. "And now"—Marion dropped her hands below her waist—"they are down here."

"They are not," Agnes said in disbelief

"They are. I swear they are," Marion answered.

"They're not."

"They are."

"They are not. Marion Delany, you shut up. You're making it up."

"They are, Agnes. I swear. Me mammy says that Tessie has to pull down her knickers to scratch her nipples. I swear."

"That's horrible," Agnes said.

"I know. I asked me mother why they hang down like that. And she said that me Auntie Tessie breast-fed her kids . . . in bunk beds." Marion laughed.

"Oh, Marion Delany, you're horrible." But Agnes howled with laughter too.

Over the next few months, as she monitored her own breasts' growth in the mirror, Agnes thought a lot about Marion's Auntie Tessie.

"Happy Birthday, dear Dolly, Happy Birthday to you." Everybody clapped except Agnes. When Agnes saw Dolly for the first time, bundled in her mother's arms, she had known straight away this baby would be trouble. In the following eight years, her opinion had changed little. Dolly had upstaged every event in Agnes' life. Dolly had been born in May, so there were rarely other events surrounding her birthday, the result of that being she got the best of gifts. Agnes, on the other hand, being born in December, tended to get a smaller gift and was pawned off with the annual statement "Sure you'll get a big gift from Santa at Christmas, won't you? And that's only a couple of weeks away."

Now this. Just eight years old, and Dolly was having a birthday

party with lots of little girls and boys from the street invited in and
given Orange Squash and sweeties. Agnes, now twelve years of age,
had yet to have a party. She was always told, "It's too close to
Christmas, darling." In honor of Dolly's birthday, Agnes was allowed to bring one friend to the party. Needless to say, that one
friend was Marion Delany. At the end of the "Happy Birthday"
song, Agnes looked over at Marion, who bent over pretending to
put her fingers down her throat and get sick. Agnes giggled.

"Okay, children, let's play some games!" Connie announced,
and the tiny children squealed. Marion whistled across the room to
get Agnes' attention, and when she had it she nodded toward the
door, signaling a quick exit. Agnes nodded back and made her way
over to Connie.

"Mammy, I'm going out with Marion, just for a while. Is that
okay?"

"Well, I was hoping you'd stay for the party, Agnes, but, okay, go
on if you want to. But don't be long." Agnes grabbed her coat and
made for the door.

"Thanks, Mrs. Reddin," Marion called over her shoulder. Connie didn't hear her, and at times only barely saw Marion, as some of
the younger children who were just six were already as tall as Marion, who was now fourteen. Once outside the building, the two girls
raced up the street.

"Come on, Agnes, I promised we'd meet Theresa Foley and Angela Connolly at the back lane of the buildings." Agnes quickened
her pace and the two girls ran side by side up the street. Marion and
Agnes found Theresa and Angela sitting on the "small wall" at the
back of the buildings.

"Where were youse two?" Angela called.

"Ah her sister's birthday party. Yuck!" The teenagers laughed.

"What's that?" Marion asked, pointing to a dark-brown bottle
beside Angela's leg. Angela and Theresa smiled slowly.

"It's drink."

"What kind of drink?" Agnes asked.

"I don't know. I think it's whiskey." She held the bottle up to the light. "It's half full." It was actually a bottle of tawny sherry that Angela had stolen from her mother's bedside cabinet. Angela's father would get the blame. Theresa took the bottle from Angela and, twisting the cork, pulled it out of the neck of the bottle with a *pop*. She held up the open bottle. "So—who's first, then?"

Agnes spun away from the bottle. "Yuck. Not me. I don't even like the smell of it!"

Of course Marion Delany's arm stretched out straight away. "Gimme it," she said, and she wiped the neck of the bottle with the palm of her hand. Without even smelling it, she put the neck to her lips and downed a gulp.

"Oh, fuck." She spat. "It tastes like medicine. Ugh!" Then she stood up straight, waited a moment, and said, "It makes your tummy feel warm, though. It's not bad."

The three girls went in turn taking mouthfuls as Agnes looked on. By the time the bottle was emptied, it was Agnes who was running from one to another holding the girls' hair out of their faces as they vomited up the sherry. They would never forget this day, these young girls. And the more distant it became, the better the memory would be, but right now it was pale faces, dry retching, and three brittle little girls.

CHAPTER FOURTEEN

It was Mrs. Brady from number 26 that had told Bosco. He had been making his way back from a late-running union meeting about the ongoing strike and the lack of progress. She ambushed him at the corner of his own street and told him the whole story.

"A bottle of sherry, a bottle of Jaysus sherry! At their age, it's disgraceful! That's what it is. I'm sure now that any of those men down on that picket line would love a bottle of sherry." Her voice was a little excited, as is the voice of any busybody who can't wait to tell a parent about an errant child. Her dig at him over the strike didn't half hurt either.

"And you're sure my daughter Agnes was there?" Bosco asked.

"Positive," said Aul Brady, and she counted the names off on her fingers. "That young O'Sullivan one with the arse out of her knickers, that one Marion Delany, and your young wan, Agnes. It was them, all right."

"Well, thanks very much for telling me, Mrs. Brady," Bosco said, tipped his hat, and smiled at the lady. "I'll look after it, thank you." He walked on, but he had forced the smile, he was angry. The thought of his little girl at just twelve years of age drinking down a lane, made him furious.

• • • • •

Connie was at the cooker stirring a pot of stew, and the girls were sitting at the table doing homework, when the fury of the man of the house fell upon them. Bosco didn't so much as enter the room as explode. He slammed the door behind him and walked just four strides to the center of the main room. The family were startled, and all eyes were on him. Immediately Agnes knew. She knew so many things all at once. She knew that somebody had told her father of her little session that day. She knew she would not get an opportunity to tell her father that, although present, she had not taken any drink. She knew that, even if she did get the opportunity to tell him that she had not taken a drink, he wouldn't believe her. She knew she was done for. The blood drained from her face.

"What's wrong, Bosco?" Connie asked with a tremor in her voice.

Bosco held up his arm. His palm was flat toward his wife. Then he shouted. "You stay out of this, woman. And *you*"—he pointed directly at Agnes—"step out here in front of me." Agnes began to rise from the table unsteadily and her eyes filled.

Connie intervened. "Now, wait a minute, Bosco. I'm entitled to an explanation here," she began, but was halted once again by Bosco's upturned arm.

"You are entitled, are you? Entitled??? Entitled to what? I, woman, am entitled." He beat his chest. "I am entitled to have my children minded properly, that's what I am entitled to. I'm entitled to know what's going on in my own home without having to hear it from neighbors on the street. That's what I'm entitled to, missus," Bosco screamed at her.

Connie advanced on Bosco. "Now, just wait a minute, Bosco. You calm down and lower your voice before you talk to anyone in this house." The slap was so rapid and made such a crack of a noise that it startled Connie before she knew she had even been slapped. Her head spun. She froze. She put her hand to her glowing red cheek.

Without a word she went to her bedroom. Agnes was now standing in front of her father screaming at him.

"I didn't even have anything to drink," she squealed, "not a drop."

"Don't you lie to me, young wan," Bosco screamed.

At the table Dolly's eyes widened as she saw it happen. It was as if it were in slow motion. Her father's right hand came across from his left hip, the back of the hand striking Agnes square across her cheek. Her head swung slightly, and the child staggered backward. Dolly began to cry. Agnes ran to the armchair and buried her face in the cushion.

Bosco stomped around the room yelling, and then stepped up behind Agnes. He bent over her; there was still fury in his voice. "Now, young wan, I hope you're happy. Look what you've caused. Your sister's upset, your mother's upset. I hope your little drinking binge was worth it. Jesus Christ, little did I know I was rearing a"— he searched—"tramp." Bosco, now at a loss for words, angrily paced the room twice and then left the flat, slamming the door behind him. And then there was silence.

Dolly, sobbing, got down from her chair and walked to the armchair where her older sister was sobbing. She slapped Agnes on the back and cried.

"You made Daddy angry and you made Mammy cry. Bitch!"

Two hours later, the two young girls were lying awake in their beds when they heard the front door open and close.

"Daddy's back," Dolly whispered.

"Shut up," Agnes said.

"Don't make him angry again, Agnes," Dolly whispered.

"I didn't make him angry. Now, shut up." Agnes had long finished her cry. "Anyway," she continued, "he'll be sorry when I'm gone away."

"I won't," Dolly said as she pulled the blanket up under her chin.

They lay there in silence for a while. Listening. There was no sound coming from outside. So the girls spoke in whispers.

"Where are you going away to?" Dolly asked Agnes.

"Canada. I told you before, I'm going to Canada. Now, shut up."

"Oh yeh, Canada. Is Canada far away, Agnes?" Dolly asked.

"I don't know, more than a hundred miles, I think."

"Daddy won't let you go, I betcha."

"He can't stop me once I'm eighteen," Agnes answered with authority.

"And when you're eighteen, Agnes, what age will I be?" Dolly asked, and Agnes thought about this for a moment, counting the years in her head.

"Thirteen." Agnes gave Dolly the answer. Dolly lay thinking about this for some moments.

"When you're eighteen, you can come to Canada after me, if you want."

"Nah. I better stay here and look after Daddy," Dolly quietly said, and she pulled the covers even tighter under her chin.

Bosco stood in the center of the room. Connie, who had been sitting in the armchair when he entered, rose and walked passed him toward the cooker.

"I'll heat your dinner. Sit down," she said. Bosco removed his cap and his jacket and tossed them onto the armchair.

"Thanks," he said simply, and sat. When the stew was reheated, Connie filled a bowl and buttered two slices of bread to accompany it. She placed the bowl and bread in front of Bosco along with the spoon. Instead of returning to the armchair, she sat at the table facing her husband. She didn't speak. Bosco began to eat, uncomfortably. After a couple of mouthfuls he put the spoon down, slowly.

"She was drinking, Agnes was. Twelve years of age and she was drinking. Down a lane with those tramp friends of hers."

"Was she?" Connie simply asked.

"*Yes*, she was. Mrs. Brady told me so," Bosco offered as evidence.

"Did she, now?" Connie asked sarcastically. "And if Mrs. Brady told you that Hitler was your father, would you come home here now and have us all goose-marching around the sitting room?"

"Don't be so silly. Why would the woman say it if it weren't the truth?"

"Because she's a lazy, idle, good-for-nothing busybody gossip who thinks there's no steam from her own shite. That's why!" Connie leaned her arms on the table. "Now, you listen to me, Mr. Big Fucking Union Man, I know the scent of me own children. I could pick them out of a crowd in an unlit coal mine. If that girl was drinking today, I'd have smelled it. And I smelled nothing!" Her voice lowered. "Which is more than can be said for you, Bosco Reddin." Connie rose from the table and walked to the cooker, over her shoulder firing a one-word question: "Tea?"

Bosco put his head in his hands and began to weep like a little baby. Connie went back to the table and stood over the slumped figure that she knew at heart was a good man. She ran her fingers through his hair.

"I was angry," Bosco sobbed, "I was disappointed." He looked up into her face. Connie placed her hand beneath her husband's chin and looked into his eyes.

"No. Not disappointed. You were scared, Bosco. You were terrified. Your little baby girl will be a teenager in less than a year, and like every father before you and those that will come after, you were scared." Bosco began to nod his head, and now the tears flowed freely down his face. Connie stooped and took his head on her shoulder and let him cry like a little boy. She brushed the back of his head softly, saying, "There, there, there," as she would to a child. A *child*, she thought. Was this man of hers ever a child? She stood there holding on to him for dear life until the high-pitched sound of the kettle as it whistled interrupted them. Connie released Bosco from her arms.

"That union will be the death of you," Connie muttered as she filled Bosco's billycan with tomato soup.

"Give us a bit of bread with that," Bosco asked, ignoring her words. He was busy lining the inside of his jacket with newspaper. It was going to be a long, cold night; the newspaper would provide much-needed insulation and heat.

"Is there no one else that can do a night picket except you?" Connie asked, not giving up. She was now buttering the thick slices of batch loaf. Again Bosco ignored her.

"Is there a heel in that?" Bosco asked. Connie held the heel, the end cut of the loaf and the thickest slice, up in the air where Bosco could see it. She offered it as evidence.

"Thanks." Bosco smiled again and winked.

"I'm serious, Bosco, it can't be just you all of the time." Connie was not just idly moaning, she was genuinely upset. Bosco saw this and walked to her. He slid his arms around her waist from behind. Gently he kissed the back of her head and closed his eyes as Connie's distinct scent filled his nostrils. When he spoke to her his voice was soft.

"Do you remember that first time you saw me speak, Connie? It was in the Gravediggers Pub," he asked and answered.

"Yes, I do," Connie answered. She closed her eyes and leaned her head back so that both their cheeks touched. "Young Liam Casey's funeral, Lord rest him," she added.

"Wasn't I brilliant, Connie?" he asked. And felt her cheek swell as a smile broke on her lips.

"Fishing for compliments, are we now?" She scorned him, but playfully.

"No, love, I just want you to remember it, and remember it well. Because on that day and in that speech I made promises. Standing beside the dead young boy's father, I made promises, and I aim to keep those promises, Connie. No matter if that means standing with the men to whom I made them throughout every night, in any weather, on any picket. Can you understand that, love? Can you, Connie?" She turned, defeated. And they kissed. When the kiss ended she held on to her man, tightly, and he to her. She whispered, "Kiss the girls good night before you go; they're awake, and upset." And they parted.

CHAPTER FIFTEEN

Bosco stood outside the girls' bedroom for a few moments. He could hear his daughters talking softly. He waited a moment to compose himself. In the girls' bedroom the conversation was very serious. Agnes, still with her back to Dolly, had tried to ignore her, but there was no escaping her sister's chat.

"When you go to Canada, the wolves will eat you," Dolly announced.

"No, they won't." Agnes was tired and sleepy.

Dolly, however, was in the wide-awake club. "They will. Wolves can smell if you're afeared, and they eat you then," Dolly insisted. Agnes didn't reply. Dolly went on. "They start with your tummy, because that's the softest part." Dolly now began to mimic wolves eating. "*Chomp, chomp,* and your belly's gone." Dolly licked her lips. "Mmmmm, they'll say, that was nice; now we'll eat her diddies."

Agnes turned. "Will you shut up?" With the onset of early puberty, Agnes was the only child in sixth class with breasts—or "diddies," as Dolly, and most young girls, referred to them—and she was not at all happy about it. Especially after Marion's story about her Auntie Tessie's drooping mammaries. The bedroom door squeaked open slowly. A crack of light shone across the room onto their bed. Framed in the light stood the silhouette of the girls' father. Dolly sat up. Agnes, still smarting from her father's slap, turned back to the wall. Bosco walked in and sat on the edge of the bed.

"I just came in to say good night to my girls," Bosco said softly.

Dolly stood in the bed and wrapped her arms around her father's neck. "Good night, Daddy," she squealed. Bosco hugged his youngest girl, and as he did so, he had his eyes on Agnes' back.

"Good night, Aggie," he said to her back.

"Good night," he received in reply without her moving. Bosco held Dolly away from him and frowned at her.

"Are you getting skinny, Dolly Reddin?" he asked, pretending concern.

"Am I, Daddy?" Dolly asked, quite serious.

Bosco looked her over and put a finger to his lips in thought. "I don't know." He snapped his fingers. "Just in case, you best go out to your mammy and get a piece of bread and butter, with sugar on it."

"Yes, please," Dolly squealed, and was gone through the open door like a ferret, calling to her mother, "Mammy! Bread! Daddy said so."

When she was gone, Bosco stretched out his arm and touched Agnes on the shoulder. She winced.

"I'm sorry, chicken," he said.

"Okay," she answered, but still did not move.

"I really am sorry, Agnes." Bosco was close to tears.

"Doesn't matter," Agnes answered, again without turning.

"Yes, it does. I know I hurt you, and I know you're in a place right now where it's hard to forgive me. I slapped you because I didn't know what else to do. I was scared." Bosco was crumbling a little bit now. Even with her back turned to him, Agnes was becoming embarrassed.

"Shut up, Da, it doesn't matter." She wanted him to stop.

"Okay, love." He rubbed her back gently and got up from the bed. At the door he turned and spoke. When he did, his voice was earnest.

"Agnes, I will never slap you again."

Hearing this, Agnes turned and looked across the room into her father's face. "Or Mammy," she insisted. "You'll never slap Mammy." She was her father's daughter.

Bosco bowed his head. "Never."

"Promise?"

"I promise you, chicken."

"Okay." Agnes smiled. "Good night, Daddy."

"Good night, my little darling." Bosco smiled and left the room.

Neither Agnes Reddin nor her mother would ever be slapped by Bosco again. But for all the wrong reasons.

CHAPTER SIXTEEN

Outside of the Parker-Willis Foundry, despite the damp and cold, the strikers were in an unusually buoyant mood. Earlier, some horse-and-carts had arrived at the picket with a gift from members of the Irish Confectioners Union. The bakers from the Johnston, Mooney, and O'Brien Bakery, on the far side of the river, had sent a huge load of two-day-old bread and half-stale cake down to the strikers. Those on picket duty filled their pockets to bring the food home. They were now munching on some of the old but tasty jam doughnuts. To the striking foundry workers, the bread and cakes meant much more than food. It was a show of support from union members in a completely different industry to their own, and knowing that the support was there was enough to bring high spirits to the picket line. There were about thirty men on the night picket this night. They had gotten some old oil barrels and punched holes in them. Full of blazing wood, they made fine braziers. There was no shortage of wood or scraps of coal along the docks. The men stood in groups around the barrels, their smiling faces lit, and warm, and there was the odd bout of laughter as stories were exchanged.

On the far side of the wall, the mood was very different. The full moon hung over the foundry, and beneath it within the yard were many more men. These men stood in large groups. As orders were whispered from one group to another, there were nods of understanding.

As Bosco turned into the street leading down to the foundry's main gates, he noticed two things. First, for the first time since they had started the picket, there were no police. None. Second, where there would usually be thirty to forty men on the night picket, this night there were at least five times that many.

Tommy Mangan met Bosco with the news and explanation of at least the second part.

"Scabs?" Bosco asked, a little puzzled. "Are you sure?" Mangan nodded his head. He was adamant. The early shift, he told Bosco, had seen over a hundred men being brought in by truck through the main gates. Bosco mulled this over.

"What'll we do?" Mangan asked, breaking into Bosco's thoughts.

"Nothing for the moment." Bosco was uneasy. "Let me think." Very uneasy. Something wasn't right. He began barking out orders:

"Tommy, get all of the marshals together. I want to talk to them. Tell everybody to keep calm until I sort this out. All right?" Mangan nodded and was gone.

Something is so not right, Bosco thought. *But . . . what is it? Something is missing?* It was not unusual for employers to bring in scab workers in an effort to break a strike. On the contrary, it was to be expected. But usually this was done in daylight, when there would be the greatest number of strikers about to see it. It was a tactic the employers used to intimidate the hard-line strikers and to scare the borderline workers into thinking they would lose their jobs. But why at night? And why *sneak* them in?

Bosco was truly puzzled, but in the meantime he had more pressing matters: controlling his own members. When Tommy

Mangan and the twenty or so marshals gathered around him, Bosco spoke to them. They listened intently to his every word.

"I'm not quite sure what Parker-Willis is up to here. But, whatever happens, we've got to keep our side in order." He looked at their faces. "Have any of you been drinking?" Three of the marshals slowly raised their hands. "Okay, you three go home now," Bosco ordered.

"What?" came a protest.

"Look, if there is any trouble here, I don't want the police to be describing us in the newspapers as a drunken rabble, okay? So go. Go now!" They left. "The rest of you, circulate among the men that are here and smell every breath. Anyone who has the slightest whiff of alcohol, send them home. Is that clear?" They nodded. They were not happy about it, but they nodded.

"Then what?" one man asked.

"I don't know yet," Bosco answered, the concern obvious in his voice. "We wait. We wait and see what happens." The men dispersed. Bosco was still uneasy. Within half an hour, anybody with drink even a sip of taken was gone home. But it made little difference. The word was now spreading throughout the tenements that the scabs had arrived at the foundry, and by daybreak the picket had swelled to over three hundred men. The marshals had given up smelling breaths, and Bosco could see that they were having difficulty controlling the crowd. He ordered a couple of the marshals to build a makeshift husting. They cobbled a stage of sorts together with a couple of barrels and a plank. Bosco climbed onto it and began trying to speak to the men.

It was now 6:45 a.m.

After he shouted for some minutes for attention, whispers of "hush" began to spread through the crowd, and they went quiet. They looked to Bosco.

"Good morning, brothers," Bosco began. "Well, now, if Mr.

Parker-Willis wants to know for sure if we are united in this strike action, he need only look out of his window this morning!" This brought a huge cheer and a wave of shaking fists. Bosco raised his arms for quiet, and the crowd hushed again. He went on. "I would indeed like him to see this"—Bosco waved his arm across the crowd as he bellowed—"but I would like him also to see a group of workingmen that behaves with dignity and honor." This got a few grumbles.

"They're fucking scabs!" a voice from the back of the gathering roared, bringing an even louder cheer from the crowd.

Bosco waved his hands for quiet again.

It was now 6:58 a.m.

Eventually the crowd went quiet.

"Listen to me. Please, listen to me," Bosco implored. Suddenly there was a *thud* sound. It came from the inside of the twenty-foot steel doors, the entrance to the foundry. All heads swiveled toward the doors. There was absolute quiet, except for the squeak of foot-steps on a wooden ladder. All eyes were now on the steel gates. Suddenly a head popped up over the top of the gates. Seeing what they believed to be one of the scabs, the crowd now went wild, screaming at the peeking head. A brick was thrown at the gates. It hit nowhere near the man on the ladder, but the bang of it hitting the gates was enough to get him to disappear. Cheers and catcalls followed the head's vanishing. It was then that it dawned on Bosco. He knew what it was that was missing. It was the squeaking of the ladder rungs that brought it home. Noise! There had been no noise. If those men were scabs, brought in to work, why could he not hear them working?

"Bully boys," Bosco said aloud, but only he heard it. "Get back," he screamed. Bosco now jumped from the husting and grabbed any marshals that were near him. "Clear the street," he screamed at them. They looked back at him with blank, puzzled faces.

"For fuck's sake, clear the street," he screamed. His voice drowned in the whistles and cheers. It was too late. At 7:00 a.m. exactly, the huge steel gates opened wide, revealing two hundred bully boys armed to the teeth. At first the strikers began to roar abuse at them, still thinking they were scab workers. But when the charge of the thugs came, the strikers got the message and bolted. Now the men at the front were trying to get away from the gates, while the men at the back of the crowd were pushing forward. The bully boys had their fish in the barrel. With adrenaline pumping, they laid into the strikers. In the mayhem that ensued, the air was filled with screams and roars of pain, and the sound of crunching as bones gave way under the heavy blows. Bosco was lifting and dragging fallen men from the ground all around him and pushing them toward the other end of the street. He screamed at them, *"Run!"* In his own ears he could hear the sound of his dying father's voice whispering, "Run, Bosco. Run, son." But he ignored it. A young man scrambling caught Bosco's eye. He looked no more than twenty years of age. The boy was doing all right at first. Terrified, he was dodging blows from a chasing bully boy wielding a pickax handle with a six-inch nail hammered through the end of it. The young man skipped and ducked as the chasing bully boy swung the club with ease. All of this time, the young man was putting a little more distance between himself and his pursuer. Then the young man tripped and fell, and as he did Bosco recognized him. It was young Mick O'Malley, the bell-ringer. He had tripped over the body of an elderly man who was lying bleeding on the road. The bully boy saw his chance. He advanced on the young Mick. With an angry roar, Bosco advanced on the bully boy. Bosco got there first. He shoulder-charged the big man and sent him sprawling and tumbling across the street. Bosco then knelt beside Michael. He helped him to his feet. The young man was terrified. Bosco looked into his face.

"Run, son. Go on, Michael lad, run," Bosco roared. O'Malley's eyes widened with fear as he saw the club come down on Bosco's head. Two inches of the nail sank into Bosco's skull. As Bosco slowly toppled forward, Michael O'Malley ran for his life.

The newspapers the following day reported the attack. They said the "incident" was the result of the actions of a drunken group of strikers attacking the legitimately hired labor force of the Parker-Willis Foundry. The eighteen men that died did so, the paper said, because of the trampling of the rabble. There were to be no post-mortems held.

Connie read this as she sat in the waiting room of the Richmond Hospital. She sat in silence and shock. The waiting-room door opened. Connie looked to the door in the hope that it was a doctor coming with news of her husband. It wasn't. It was instead a pale-faced young boy. He introduced himself as Michael O'Malley; he was twenty years old, he said, and had been saved, he told Connie, by the intervention of her husband. He had been told that the man was taken here.

"How is he?" the boy asked.

"I don't know, son, I don't know," Connie answered the boy. She was numb. The boy placed his hand upon hers and began to re-cite aloud the Lord's Prayer. Connie neither felt his hand nor heard his words. When he finished the prayer, the boy removed a gold chain and crucifix from about his neck. He tried to put this into Connie's hand. Her hand would not grasp it, just as her mind could not grasp the horror of the past twelve hours. So the boy wrapped the chain around her thumb.

"Missus, please tell your husband that if I can ever do anything for him he need just ask." Connie did not respond. The boy stroked her hand and sat quietly beside Connie and waited. He saw the newspaper lying on the table and turned it toward himself. He read only the headline.

"Good God, eighteen dead." The boy sighed. The waiting-room door opened. It was about to be nineteen. Connie collapsed.

Michael O'Malley left the hospital in a teary daze and walked and walked. And walked.

CHAPTER SEVENTEEN

The year that followed her father's death was a slow one for young Agnes. The first couple of weeks following the funeral were not too bad. There had been lots of callers to the flat, and the entire neighborhood had expressed its sympathy to the Reddin family. Then, one day, everybody just stopped calling. As is life, they all went back to what they had been doing, and within months the riot and, with it, the death of Bosco Reddin were virtually forgotten.

Things became decidedly uncomfortable for Geoffrey Parker-Willis, so within months of the "Misery Hill Massacre" the foundry had been sold to a Liverpool shipbuilding company, and the entire Parker-Willis family had immigrated to South Africa. Not until they were well gone did Constance tell Agnes who her grandparents had been. It was a dreadful shock for the young girl. She had always believed that she had no grandparents on her mother's side. Killed in the Great War or something, her mother had said. Now, to be told that they had lived within miles of her was one shock; to discover not only that she did have a grandfather but that he had killed her father, left the child numbed and confused. Constance had taken it all dreadfully. She now sat for long periods in silence. She lost so much weight that her skin seemed just to hang from her bones. She also lost interest completely in her daughters. So Agnes became head of the house, a job she didn't want. The last thing Constance did for either of her girls was to cut the train of her wedding dress for the final time to make Dolly's Communion dress. Feeling the fabric of the dress she wore for the man she so deeply loved, broke her heart. She cried over every stitch, but, still, when she had finished it Dolly's dress was beautiful. The only good thing for Agnes about this year was that it was her last one in school. She thought June 29 would never arrive, but it did.

As Agnes had expected, Marion was not in class for the final day of school. Sister Benedict was just as happy as Marion was that Marion wasn't there. The nun had prepared her "into the big bad world" speech but unfortunately never got to deliver it. As it transpired, the final day of school for the rest of the girls in the sixth class was to end early when the school fire alarm went off. It was a young nun, Sister Loretta, that had seen the smoke billowing from the corner of the school shed. All of the children were evacuated from the building, and the fire truck was there within minutes. It turned out to be just a small fire, a bundle of books, the shed door, and the remains of a battered leather satchel. The children crowded around the shed to get a look, but Agnes instead scanned the streets surrounding the school until she saw her. Marion was standing half hidden in a doorway. Agnes waved to her and Marion waved back and with a huge smile Marion blew a kiss to the school and ran off up the street.

For most of the girls in that class of 1947, the last day of school that year was to be their last day of all schooling. Needless to say, this would be a sure thing for Marion Delany and Agnes Reddin. Also, for the first time Agnes would have no summer holidays for now it was time to get a job. Her mother was just barely scraping by on the seven-shilling pension she was getting from the State, so now Agnes could make a contribution. She looked forward to it. She spent her first couple of weeks knocking on the doors of every place of employment near the Jarro, but to no avail. Each afternoon she would finish her day in Moore Street, helping Marion pack away the Delany stall. Mrs. Delany would wrap up some potatoes or whatever vegetables were left over for Agnes to bring home to her mother and younger sister.

Each day Agnes helped out at the stall, she was being watched closely. Across from the Delany stall was the stall of Nellie Nugent. Nellie usually said nothing but watched everything. And she was watching Agnes Reddin.

It was about this time that Agnes began to see a change in her mother. Small things. Like calling Dolly Agnes or vice versa. One or two mornings, Agnes found a packed lunch for her father. This itself was strange enough to a thirteen-year-old girl, but even more strange and a little scary was that when she would bring it to her mother's attention her mother denied knowing where it had come from or what it was. If this was not enough for Agnes to deal with, Dolly was beginning to get completely out of control. With no school for the next eleven weeks, Dolly had taken to vanishing each morning and not returning until dusk, which at this time of the year was later and later each evening. Another thing, Dolly never seemed to be hungry, unlike Agnes, who couldn't wait to tuck into the shepherd's pie or stew cooked up for the "tea," as the evening meal is known to all Dubliners.

All was revealed one afternoon by Marion, albeit a bit too late. Agnes was helping Marion to dismantle the stall when, out of the blue, Marion brought up Dolly.

"You'd want to keep an eye on your sister, Agnes," Marion said as they were working away.

"What do you mean?" Agnes had been on her knees rolling up the canvas. She now stopped and stood. Marion was stacking boxes, and she continued stacking as she spoke.

"Dolly was up outside the pub last night selling leather belts, so my mammy says."

"Selling belts? For who?"

"For herself."

"Don't be stupid, Marion. Where would Dolly get leather belts?" Agnes was rooted to the spot by a mixture of puzzlement and shock.

"She steals them, Agnes," Marion revealed. Now the puzzlement was gone but not the shock. Agnes couldn't speak. Marion stopped stacking boxes. "There's a gang of them." She began to rhyme off the names, counting them on her fingers. "Sadie Scully, Maggie O'Hare, Nuala Wade, and a few others. They go shoplifting during the day, and then they sell the stuff outside the pubs at night." Once this was said, Marion went straight back to work.

Agnes immediately became defensive. "Shoplifting? Shoplifting? It's that Sadie Scully one. I bet she put Dolly up to it. Dolly would never do anything like that unless she was being led to it." Marion went to answer this but then thought better of it. Agnes saw her hesitation and goaded her. "What? Marion, come on, what?" Agnes had her hands on her hips now. Marion stacked the last box, and as she was wiping her hands in her apron she said, "Agnes, they call the gang 'Dolly's Mixtures.' Do you think Sadie came up with that too?"

Agnes turned on her heel.

"Aggie, wait," Marion called after her, but she didn't look back.

As Agnes rounded a corner into her street it was like a nightmare. She was already upset and worried about what Marion had said, but her stomach now dropped to her toes and the blood drained from her body. She froze and threw up with fright. The police car was parked right outside her building. A small crowd had gathered around it, and as Agnes got closer she knew the police car was for Dolly. One kid saw Agnes arrive and sang at her: "Your sister's going to prison, your sister's going to prison. Ha. Ha. Ha."

Agnes took the steps up to her flat two at a time. She didn't realize as she climbed that she was running into the most bizarre twist in her life. Things would never be the same again.

"Who's this, now? Is this one of the other girls? Tell me, you little brat." the policeman barked at Dolly in a thick country accent when Agnes entered the room. Dolly was sitting on one of the fireside chairs in a fetal position. Her eyes were red raw from crying, her arms red from slaps. The huge policeman sat on the other fireside chair. Agnes' mother, Connie, was sitting at the table. Both Connie and the policeman had cups of tea, and Agnes was shocked when her mother, instead of intervening on her behalf, said, "Dolly, answer the policeman—is this one of the other girls?"

"No, that's my sister," Dolly answered.

Agnes walked slowly toward her mother. "Mammy? Are you all right, Mammy?" Agnes stood in front of her mother.

"Is it, missus? Is that your daughter?" the policeman asked. He spoke to Connie in a little more civil tone.

"Yes, it is indeed, and this is also my daughter Agnes," Connie replied.

"Mammy, what's going on?" Agnes asked, confused.

"It's all right, dear, sit down, everything is going to be all right, we'll sort this out," Connie answered Agnes in a very kind voice.

"But, Mammy . . ." Agnes began, but was cut off by the policeman. "Do what your mother tells you, yeh little bitch, or you'll get a clout from me," he barked. Agnes sat. For one half-hour they all sat there in silence. Had Dolly not let out a little sob and whimper, they would probably still be sitting there now.

"Oh, go on, cry now, you little pup, ya," the policeman broke the silence in response to Dolly's cry. That's when Connie spoke, and for Agnes the world changed.

"Don't worry, Garda, my husband will straighten all this out when he gets in from work." Slowly the two daughters looked over toward their mother in simultaneous disbelief. "I used to have a maid, you know," Connie said to the officer.

CHAPTER EIGHTEEN

I t must have been pity. For, once the policeman was told that Connie's husband would not be home that afternoon or indeed any other afternoon, his whole manner and demeanor changed. He sent for an ambulance for Agnes' mother, and once Connie was admitted to the Mater Hospital he even drove the two girls home. On the way, of course, he gave Dolly a stern lecture on the evils of crime and warned her that she was so close to being sent to a home for "bad" girls. This home for bad girls, from his description, was two bus stops past hell. Anyhow, Dolly swore on her father's grave that she would never get in trouble again, and when the policeman was gone, Agnes was still in too much shock and fear even to talk to Dolly. They both fell asleep in the armchairs by the fire.

The next morning, Agnes awoke to find herself the woman of the house. At thirteen years of age, she had a home to run and a young child to rear. The day went downhill from there, for by lunchtime the hospital had discharged Connie with a handful of sedatives, realizing that they could medically do no more. Now Agnes was to be virtually a mother of two. She did not make it down to Moore Street that day, and Marion, mistakenly thinking that she and Agnes had fallen out, didn't call until the next day. On seeing Marion, Agnes was delighted. She threw her arms around her and hugged her tightly. For the first time in two days, Agnes felt like she was not alone.

Over the next few days, Connie began to improve some, and Agnes took to the job-search trail yet again. Day after day she returned unhappily without a job, but each day found her mother getting better and better. Until, after two weeks, it was as if the incident had never happened. It was a temporary respite, but still a welcome one. After four weeks and still no job, Agnes was really beginning to despair.

"I don't know what I'll do if I don't get a job," she told Marion one day as both of them sat by the stall in Moore Street.

"I know where there's a job," Marion announced very simply.

"What?" Agnes thought she had misheard.

"I said I know where you can get a job."

"Where?"

"Here in Moore Street, working on a stall." Marion smiled and crossed her arms. Agnes smiled right back at her.

"Me? Me working on a stall? I couldn't sell," Agnes dismissed herself straight away.

"You wouldn't have to sell; well, not at first anyway. At first you just help out, build the stall in the mornings, collect stuff from the markets, clean the fruit, and at nighttime take the stall down. It's simple."

Agnes thought about it for a moment, working in Moore Street. She looked up and down this wonderfully colorful, musical street that already had been so much part of her childhood.

"But, Marion, your mother isn't busy enough to employ you and me, and she's hardly going to sack you." Even as she was speaking these words, Agnes could see an impish little look in Marion's eyes.

"It is for your mother, isn't it?" Agnes asked. Marion shook her head.

"Not your mother?" Marion shook her head again. "Then who?"

"Nellie Nugent," Marion announced. Agnes' eyes widened, her mouth opened wide, and her jaw dropped. She spun her head around to look across the street at the same Nellie Nugent.

"Nellie Nugent. Nellie Nugent with a face that could turn the tides? Nellie Nugent with an arse so big you could park your bicycle in the crack of it? Nellie Nugent with a face like a cow licking piss off a nettle?"

Marion began to giggle and laugh, for it was indeed her own descriptions of Nellie Nugent that Agnes was now reciting back to her. "Yes," she cried through the laughter. When Marion eventually stopped laughing and gathered herself, she went on to explain. "I'm sorry, Agnes, it's just that she was asking my mother who you were. You know, she says to me mam, 'Who's that girl that hangs around your stall all day, and has she nothing better to be doing?' Mammy just told her that you came here every day after you were out looking for work. So you know Nellie, she said to me mammy, 'If she wants work I'll give her work, I'll give her plenty of work.' I didn't think it would be fair not to mention it to you." Again Marion burst into laughter, and this time so did Agnes. Nellie Nugent looked across the street over her shoulder with that scowl on her face, and the two girls stopped laughing abruptly.

"Careful," Marion said through her teeth. "Me mother said that she could hear a five-pound note dropping at five hundred paces." And the two girls howled with laughter again and now had to hide behind the stall. As they crouched there, Marion became a little more serious. "Agnes, stalls here are handed down from mother to daughter. We just don't get new people in here. You mightn't think it, but it's a great honor to be asked, if she really is asking, that is."

Whether Nellie Nugent's offer of a job was genuine or not, Agnes didn't have time to think about it. For the very next day she was offered her first position. Agnes had called into Walker's Rainwear Limited, a huge sewing factory that employs nearly five hundred girls. Lo and behold, within thirty minutes of filling out her name and address on an application form, she was hired, and began work the next day, making buttonholes.

Walker's Rainwear Limited had been making gabardine rainwear and trench coats for fifteen years. They depended heavily on orders from the European mainland countries, whose military contracts kept the place going. Now they had expanded. In America the trench coat was becoming all the rage for the man in the street. Walker's was sending them over there by the boatload. The key to the success of the company was, of course, the young girls that worked for very little money. The rag trade at this time was exploitive everywhere, and if Walker's had a good side it would be fair to say that it was a little less exploitive than some. Every girl that had completed her three months' probation was given a free trench coat. The company was unionized. The girls had regular tea breaks, and the working week was only forty-five hours. Every new girl started on the buttonholer, then moved to the flat machines, then to the overlocker. The process of moving as far as the overlocker took about a year. Not for Agnes. She proved to be really adept with the machines and was overlocking by the time she received her free coat. Her wages of one pound eighteen shillings and sixpence was over five times her mother's widow's pension. So not only did life improve at home, Agnes could even spend a little on herself. After a hard week's work, Agnes' treat was to take Marion to the Metropole Cinema on Friday night. There they would sit licking their Orange Maid ice pops, and chewing away on a bar of Cleeves toffee. The two girls were enthralled by the movies, every movie—although they did have a penchant for Boris Karloff horrors. It was during the interval at one of these that Agnes was fired by an idea that she had not had since the night her father died. The usual adverts were running when suddenly the screen was filled with a scene of a forest in the fall. Technicolor at its best. The picture took Agnes' breath away. Brown, gold, red, orange, green, and blue. It was stunning. Then came the smiling faces of happy people, big cars, fashionable clothes. And the voice-over. *"Your new life awaits you in beautiful Canada."* Canada! Agnes' eyes opened wide.

Marion frowned. "Canada? Where's that?" she asked Agnes.

"Beside Greenland," Agnes answered without taking her eyes from the screen.

Marion shrugged. "I'm no fuckin' wiser now." She went back to licking her lolly.

Agnes watched and listened. *"Call in and talk to us at the Canadian Embassy and soon you too could be on your way to the most beautiful country in the British Empire. Assisted passage is only twenty pounds. We need people just like you."* And then it was gone. The picture, but not the idea.

From the public phone outside the canteen in Walker's, Agnes made the call the following Monday. The girl in the Canadian Embassy sounded really nice. She told Agnes that there were plenty of jobs available in Canada and described how beautiful Toronto, her own home, was. She took Agnes' address and told her the application for assisted passage would arrive by post within days. She didn't, however, ask Agnes her age. To Agnes' delight, the letter arrived from the Canadian Embassy two days later. She did not open it until that night. Her mother was asleep, and Dolly, back to her wayward ways, had still not arrived home. The flat was quiet, and she spread the papers over the table. There was lots of information, but only one form to fill out, Agnes was glad of that. She began answering the questions, filling in the answers as neatly as she could, in pencil. It took her over an hour to finish. She read it over and over again, and when she was satisfied she had done her best, she sealed the prepaid envelope and left the flat to post it straight away. As Agnes was coming down the stairs she could hear the thud of heavy feet coming up. On the next landing she met the policeman.

"Do you live here, in this building?" the policeman asked her.

"Yes," she said. And she knew.

"Do you know the Reddins?" he asked.

CHAPTER NINETEEN

Agnes' heart was breaking. Marion squeezed her hand. Dolly looked tiny, standing there before the judge, flanked by two huge policemen. The arresting officer gave his account of the burglary. He was convinced, he said, that there were at least three young wans involved. However, the one he caught, Dolly, refused to give any other names. Dolly looked over her shoulder at her sister. Both were close to tears, and yet they smiled at each other. The judge, a severe-looking woman with her glasses halfway down her nose, stared at the child. She tut-tutted and looked around the room.

"Is the child's father here?" she asked the room.

"No, he's dead." It was Agnes that spoke. The judge looked at her.

"And who might you be, young lady?" she asked.

"I'm *her* sister." Agnes said this with pride.

"And I'm *her* friend," said Marion.

"Shut up, Marion," Agnes said from the corner of her mouth.

"Okay," Marion said back.

"Is your mother here, then?" The judge was moving swiftly along. There were a lot more children to be judged today.

"No. Me mammy couldn't come, she's sick," Agnes lied. She had not told her mother, for fear that it would kill her.

"What am I to do with you, little girl? Eh, what am I to do?" The judge waited for Dolly to reply. Dolly said nothing.

"Any previous?" the judge asked the policeman. He shook his head. "All right, three years' probation." She looked at Dolly. " Do you understand what that means?"

"No, ma'am," Dolly answered softly.

"If I see you here again within the next three years, I will send you to a place so far away that nobody will hear you scream. And you *will* scream!"

Outside the court, Dolly wrapped her arms around her sister. They cried loudly.

"Don't you ever bring me here again, do you hear me, Dolly Reddin!" Agnes sobbed.

"I won't, Aggie, I'm sorry. I swear I won't." Dolly held on to her sister for dear life. The three walked home from the court. Well, Agnes and Dolly were going home, but Marion was going to work, so the girls walked her to Moore Street on their way home. When they got to the stall, Mrs. Delany was livid.

"Where were you?" she screamed at Marion. Marion was about to tell her, then caught the worried look on Agnes' face.

"Nowhere," she answered.

"Well, I had to build this stall meself. I had to rack it out meself. What the fuck do you think you're at? I got no breakfast, no break, I haven't even had time to scratch me arse!" She caught Marion with a slap on the back of the head.

"I'm sorry," Marion said, close to tears. Her mother's slap had hurt.

"Sorry, is it? Oh, I feel much better now. Sure the hunger's gone now. I'll give you fuckin' sorry, miss." She swung again but Marion moved away from the slap this time. Agnes and Dolly moved even farther away. Suddenly Marion let fly.

"Well, now you know how hard I have to work. I've been building that stall since I was seven, and not once did you say thanks, not once," she yelled at her mother. Mrs. Delany went purple with rage. She lunged at Marion, but Marion began to run around the stall. Her mother gave chase, screaming: "Stand still till I hit yeh, yeh bloody bitch." Marion took off down the street. Her mother wasn't going that far. She stopped, breathless.

"Yeh little wagon!" she roared. "Don't come back!" Mrs. Delany turned and saw some other dealers and customers looking at her. "What are youse fuckin' lookin' at?" she screamed at them. They went back to their business.

Agnes took Dolly by the hand. "Come on, let's find her," she said, and the two ran after Marion.

Marion was not the least bit contrite. "She's a lazy old bitch." She was angry.

"Maybe she's just in bad humor?" Agnes offered.

"Ah, she's always in bad humor. She doesn't even pay me. I have to rob money when she's not looking." Marion was walking behind Agnes and Dolly.

"What will you do?" Agnes asked.

"I dunno." Marion hung her head. "Can I sleep in your flat, Agnes? Will you ask your mammy?"

"I don't have to ask. Come on, let's go home." The three walked side by side, all holding hands. Such a grown-up day for these three children.

That night, Marion shook Agnes awake. Agnes looked at her in wonderment for a moment. She had forgotten Marion was staying there.

"What's wrong, Marion?" Agnes wiped the sleep from her eyes. Marion, on the other hand, looked wide awake.

"I have an idea." Marion was excited.

"Tell me in the morning." Agnes lay back down.

"No. Listen," Marion insisted.

"Go on, then, what is it?" Agnes agreed to listen, but she was not rising again.

"I'll work with you."

"What?"

"In the sewing factory, I'll get a job there. We'll be together every day. What do you think?" Marion had it all figured out.

"Okay. I'll ask in the morning," Agnes said sleepily. She pulled the blanket over herself and went back to sleep. Marion lay awake, smiling.

Marion lasted just one day in the sewing factory. She did not like the work. She did not like being cooped up in the sweaty building. She called it school with sewing machines. She did not like the other girls. From the moment she arrived with Agnes that morning, some of the other girls were already eyeing her suspiciously. At the timekeeper's office, Marion was stopped and asked to produce her birth certificate. The timekeeper read over the certificate and eyed Marion up and down.

"So this is really *your* certificate?" he asked.

"Yes, it is," Marion answered sternly; she did not like authority at all.

"Well, you don't look fifteen." The man's eyes narrowed as he spoke.

"And you don't look like an arsehole, so who can tell?" Marion answered.

"Don't cheek me, you little bitch," the man snapped. He was angry now. Agnes intervened.

"She's been passed by Personnel, mister."

The man handed Marion back her birth certificate and opened the staff book. He ran his finger down the names until he found Marion's. From a drawer he took out a fresh beige clock-in card and wrote Marion's name on the top. Then he pushed the card through the tiny window of his office. Through this little window he shouted, "Your staff number is 2185; remember that," he growled.

"I'll have it tattooed on the inside of my eyelids," Marion quipped as Agnes was dragging her away. Agnes showed Marion how to go about clocking in her card and then took her to the flat-machine room. As Marion entered the room, she gasped. "Jesus Christ."

It was a big room and it was crammed with rows upon rows of sewing machines. More than one hundred in all. Agnes took Marion to the supervisor, Mrs. Kelly, introduced them to each other, and then left Marion with the neatly dressed middle-aged woman. When Mrs. Kelly had gone over the rules with Marion (two toilet visits per day, two tea breaks, etc.), she took Marion to a machine.

It was a buttonholer, the machine everybody learned on. Mrs. Kelly sat at the machine and, with Marion looking on, began to teach her how to cut buttonholes, guiding the fabric carefully while at the same time pushing the pedal with both feet to keep the mechanics of the machine turning. Marion was a quick student, and in no time at all Mrs. Kelly had her sit down to use the machine herself. Before going back to her desk, at the top of the room, Mrs. Kelly gave Marion a sheaf of fabric squares and left the young girl there, practicing alone. There was enough space on each square for ten buttonholes. While Marion practiced away, the rhythm of a production line echoed around the rest of the room. Flat machines, overlockers, and cutters were running at full speed. The girls were all singing aloud to the songs that were playing at full volume over the Tannoy.

By the time the siren went off to signal the first tea break, Marion had made five hundred buttonholes and was bored stiff. Agnes came to find Marion and brought her to the canteen, where they lined up for a cup of tea. The tea break was allowed just fifteen minutes, and the two girls spent ten of these waiting in line. They used the remaining five minutes to drink the tea and have a quick smoke. By then the siren had sounded again. As it did, the entire room stood en masse and began to return to work. As the two girls were leaving the canteen, Marion caught Agnes by the arm.

"Aggie, I'm sorry, but I hate this place," she said apologetically.

"Give it a chance, Marion. You will like it, but you have to give it a chance," Agnes assured her.

"I won't, Agnes . . . ever," Marion said. Too late, Agnes was already gone.

Marion went back to her machine. Mrs. Kelly had left another bale of off-cuts for Marion to practice on, and Marion carried on. The lunch siren came and went, and Marion was no happier. After lunch Mrs. Kelly moved Marion to a different machine, an overlocker. Again Marion grasped the technique very quickly and was shortly running the machine at full speed and very bored. By now the smell of the machine oil mixed with the smell of the fabrics was beginning to sicken Marion. Her stomach turned and she had a headache. She told this to the girl next to her, and the girl suggested that Marion tell Mrs. Kelly.

Eileen Kelly had been employed in the rag trade for many years. She had been a good cutter, and an excellent machinist. But it was when she was promoted to supervisor that Eileen really blossomed.

She was well organized and very matronly with the girls, and they liked her for that. Girls could begin working in the sewing factory at thirteen or fourteen years, and many, many did. With the employing of immature young girls came many problems, physical and psychological. It was difficult, for instance, for a supervisor to set accurate targets, as at that age consistency was virtually nonexistent. Girls of this age often saw working as a form of play and had to be controlled, but not too sternly. On the physical side, one of the main problems that faced Eileen Kelly was that a lot of her girls were in the early stages of their first menstruation, or in some cases had not begun to menstruate at all. And so they would arrive at Eileen's desk frightened, bewildered, and confused. But Eileen was ready for every event. In the bottom left-hand drawer of her desk she kept a huge stock of sanitary towels and a jumbo box of aspirins. When a young girl would arrive at her desk pale and teary-eyed saying something like, "Mrs. Kelly, I don't feel well," Eileen would simply nod her head, tell the girl it was all right, dip her hand into the drawer of her desk, take out two aspirins, wrap them in a sanitary towel, hand them to the girl, and point to the ladies'.

This is exactly what she did when Marion arrived at her desk and told her that her stomach was sick and she had a headache. She smiled knowingly at Marion and handed her her little bundle. And so it was that Marion, who had yet to menstruate, was standing in the ladies' toilet completely confused, holding two aspirins in one hand and what resembled a white hammock in the other. Five minutes later, when Marion came out of the ladies' toilet, she passed by Mrs. Kelly's desk. As she passed, she said a mannerly "Thank you, Mrs. Kelly, I feel a bit better now." Without even looking up, Mrs. Kelly waved her hand and said, "Don't mention it, darling." Marion returned to her machine and began overlocking again. For any of the girls in the large room to get to the ladies' toilet, they had to pass by the row of machines at which Marion was sitting. Marion barely noticed the first two or three girls that went past her, tittering. But soon the girls were heading for the toilet in fours and fives, and the tittering had been replaced by unabashed laughter.

In the toilet, Marion had taken a paper cup and swallowed the two aspirins with a drop of water. However, the miniature white hammock had completely confused her. So she put her mind to work. She ran the cold tap and gently lowered the hammock into the cool water and squeezed it damp. She then put the cloth across her forehead, looping it around both ears. By the time Mrs. Kelly came down to see what all the laughter was about, Agnes had also arrived and saw her best friend sitting at the overlocker machine looking like a racehorse. Agnes virtually ran to Marion's side, whipped off the sanitary towel, and threw it away. She took Marion by the hand and Marion stood. Agnes turned to the gathering mass of girls. "You shower of bitches."

"What's wrong?" Marion asked. "What is it, what's wrong?"

"Nothing, Marion. Come on, we're leaving."

Agnes took Marion by the hand and burst through the gang of laughing girls. The rag trade had seen the last of Reddin and Delany.

CHAPTER TWENTY

The banging on the door woke everybody up. By the time Agnes had gotten out of bed, Constance was already opening it.

Mrs. Delany was very polite. Agnes recognized her voice. "I'm sorry to trouble you at this late hour, Mrs. Reddin," she apologized. Agnes ran back into the bedroom.

"It's your mother," she whispered loudly to Marion.

"I'm not here." Marion began to crawl under the bed.

Agnes could hear her mother invite Mrs. Delany into the flat. She dived to the ground and stuck her head under the bed. "She's coming in," she whispered.

"Fuck off, I'm not here," Marion insisted.

"Agnes! Agnes, come out here," Constance called.

"Ah, now, don't be getting the child out of bed on my account, Mrs. Reddin. Sure I'll go in to her," Mrs. Delany said.

"Shite, she's coming in here," Agnes whispered, scrambling under the blankets. The short, stocky woman entered the bedroom. She stopped in the doorway.

"Agnes? Are you awake, love?"

"Yes."

Mrs. Delany came to the bed and sat on the edge. Agnes sat up, holding the blankets to her chest. Dolly pretended to be asleep, but was shaking with fright.

"Agnes, I don't know where Marion is, I can't find her any-where. Now, you probably don't know either?" She waited. Agnes didn't answer.

"Anyhow, I was hoping you might bump into her, and if you do would you give her a message for me?" The woman's voice was soft and nice, and it frightened Agnes even more. She nodded her head.

"Good. Tell her that I am very sorry for being annoyed at her, and that I love her and miss her very much. Tell her that I can't manage the stall on me own and that if she will come back I'll be nicer to her."

"And pay me?" came a voice from under the bed.

The bright August sun shone down Moore Street. It was a beautiful Irish summer's day. Agnes stood beside Marion at her mother's stall. They watched Nellie and Mrs. Delany across the street, talking. Every now and then, Nellie would throw a glance over at Agnes. Each time Marion would give a commentary, "She's lookin', stand up straight," and Agnes would. They awaited the outcome of Mrs. Delany's approach on behalf of Agnes.

Nellie Nugent, in her late fifties, was a quiet, uncomplicated woman. She had been standing in the same spot in Moore Street selling vegetables every trading day for forty years, with the excep-tion of a five-year gap which she spent in prison for killing her third husband. On the evening of the man's death, Nellie had called the police to say that her husband had committed suicide. However, on arrival, just the preliminary examination of the body showed four-teen stab wounds, and this would have made it the worst case of sui-cide ever seen in Ireland. So Nellie was arrested. A subsequent inquiry revealed that David Nugent, the dead man, an ex–British Army sol-dier, had been beating on Nellie on such a regular basis that it bordered on torture. And on that particular night, Nellie had just cracked in the middle of one of his beatings. She went into a frenzy, and she told the court that once she began she found it difficult to stop. She was found guilt of manslaughter and served her time. Her plea of aggravated self-defense was not accepted, for at this time in Ireland it was indeed legal to beat your wife, provided you did not use a stick longer than your forearm. Nellie's first two husbands, both coincidentally British soldiers, had died of natural causes: they were shot, in battle, naturally.

Nellie spoke very little—no idle chitchat, no gossiping—and she rarely smiled. She knew who her friends were on Moore Street, and she was a good friend to them, but she distrusted outsiders. There were a thousand nicknames that could have been given to Nellie; "the Black Widow" or "Praying Mantis" spring to mind immediately. But this is Dublin, and more particularly this is Moore Street, where the direct approach is always found to be the best. So it was that Nellie was simply known as "Nellie the Knife." Now getting toward her sixtieth year, Nellie was tired. Forty years on the street, prison, trauma, and life had taken their toll, and it was getting harder and harder for Nellie to keep the stall going alone. Nellie had no children as far as anyone knew, and she never spoke of relatives. So, unlike all the other women on the street, who were surrounded by family that would help on the stalls, Nellie ran a solo operation.

Mrs. Delany called Agnes to come over.

"Here goes," Agnes said aloud.

"Good luck, Agnes." Marion was more nervous than Agnes.

Agnes walked briskly across the street. At the stall, she stood beside Mrs. Delany. It was time for her job interview.

Nellie looked her up and down. "Show me your hands," she asked. Agnes held her hands out, palms up.

"She's a hard worker!" Mrs. Delany offered.

"She'd better be," Nellie stated flatly. She looked Agnes in the eyes. "Don't give me any shit," she warned.

"I won't," Agnes promised.

A customer approached. Nellie tossed a couple of bright-red tomatoes into a paper bag, spun the bag around to seal it, and took the customer's money. When the customer was gone she returned to the interview. "Right, I'll try the young wan out." And the interview was over.

CHAPTER TWENTY-ONE

Marion had the key to Nellie's shed; it had been given to her by her mother the previous evening. She was told to pass it on to Agnes for her first day at work. Marion indeed passed the key over to Agnes, in what resembled a pagan ritual. The holding of the shed key carried with it great responsibility, and on handing over the key to Agnes, Marion greatly emphasized this:

"Never leave the street during trading hours with the key." Marion spoke as if these words had been drummed into her; they probably were. Agnes nodded.

"If you must leave the street, give the key to the dealer, in this case Nellie Nugent. Once you have returned to the street, get the key back immediately. Now, this is important," Marion said. "Nothing annoys a dealer more than asking her runner"—she pointed to Agnes—"you, to fetch something from the shed and then you having to ask her for the key, it drives them mad." Marion lifted her eyes to heaven, and Agnes nodded very seriously, as if she understood every word and indeed the implications of every word.

Marion continued: "Agnes, as the holder of the key, you must be on time every day, no exceptions."

Agnes nodded. "I will," she promised.

"Now, I've put the key on a bit of string that you can put around your neck. That's the best place to keep it: that way you know it's always there." Marion handed the key and string to Agnes, who immediately put it around her neck as if it were an Olympic medal. They smiled at each other.

"Right, let's get going," Marion said. Agnes' new boss, Nellie, would spend from 5 a.m. to 7 a.m. in the wholesale fruit markets. There she would be picking the best fruit and vegetables, haggling with the wholesaler, and deciding what would sell and what would not sell. There is no storage in the shed for fruit. Once the horse and cart arrive from the wholesalers, everything must go on the stall, so the stall must be ready for stocking out. The two young girls opened the shed and began to drag and carry the makings of the stall from the shed. There were four leg slats, hinge supports that opened out so a top board could lay across them to provide the table base upon which the stall would be built. In Nellie's case, her stall would be eight feet wide and four feet deep. Then three wooden apple-boxes were carried up. Two of these would be placed end to end in the center of the stall, and the third one on top of the two, giving the stall its popular triangle-ish form. Next, over the entire structure was thrown a sheet of green sacking. This would be tucked and fitted into the corners and the base of the apple boxes and held there by heavy iron bars. Agnes worked feverishly. She had helped Marion build her mother's stall many times, and indeed Nellie's was similar in shape, so she managed quite well. When she completed it, Agnes went across the street to Marion, who was busy finishing her own mother's stall.

"What do you think?" she asked Marion. Marion stopped what she was doing and ran a critical eye over Agnes' work. She smiled.

"Well done, Agnes, it looks great."

"Really? Does it, really?"

"Yeh. Brilliant. You're a natural, girl, a natural," Marion confirmed.

Agnes gave a little giggle of delight. "Will she like it, do you think?"

"What?" Marion was back working now.

"Nellie, will she like it?" Agnes was smiling.

"Oh no. No, she won't like it. Nellie doesn't like anything." And Marion carried on working. With the wind taken out of her sails, Agnes strolled back to her monument and began tidying out the area to await Nellie's arrival.

The fresh fruit, vegetable, and fish wholesale markets in Dublin City take in a huge area from Capel Street down through Mary's Abbey, from Green Street down to Strand Street and across to Church Street. The center of the market, and indeed the center of the activity, is the main Corporation Market building itself.

On the north side of the building, just across the road from the main building itself, stands Rosie's Market Café. Rosie's opens for business in the early hours of the morning, when John Joe O'Reilly unlocks the doors at 3:30 a.m. The doors stay open until the late afternoon, and its clientele come in shifts.

At 3:30 a.m. would come the prostitutes. These would arrive for their end-of-working-day snack. From that moment on, the place would be a buzz of conversation in high-pitched squeals as the gossip of the previous evening was discussed. "Crabs, says he. What? says I. Have you got crabs? says he. Yes, says I, what do you expect for two pound fucking prawns?" Squeals of laughter, slagging matches, tears, and the odd argument all happening at the same time, while John Joe O'Reilly, the proprietor and chef, would be trying to grab orders, and not in the style of the more sedate Southside restaurants. For instance, one would rarely see a chef patrone on the south side of the city scream at a customer, "I heard ya, eggs sunny side up, I'm not fucking deaf. Now sit down, you fat slapper. Next!"

By 4:30 a.m., these would be all gone, and John Joe would have time for a smoke before the 5:00 a.m. arrivals. This time, long-distance truck drivers. These hardy, tough men would have driven through the night from the four corners of Ireland to get their produce to the markets before 3 a.m. It could take up to two hours to unload their produce, and now it was time for their dinner before setting out again cross-country to reload and get some sleep. Steaming tea was served in half-pint mugs for these men, none of your fancy cups here, and the toast would be thick-cut bread dripping in melted butter. They were a reasonably quiet lot, though, preferring to use the time chewing the grease rather than chewing the fat. The drivers would leave virtually en masse before 6 a.m., the huge convoy clogging the narrow market lanes for about thirty minutes as they exited the city. For the rest of the morning, Rosie's Café belonged to the dealers.

When the dealers had finished in the wholesaler's, they would repair to Rosie's Market Café for a greasy fry-up, some tea, and some toast. Outside of Rosie's would stand the line of well-sprung prams of varying manufacturers but of similar design. Each pram would be laden down with whatever the dealer could push. This would give her the opportunity to get her stall partially stacked while she awaited the arrival of the horse and cart later in the morning. The dealers were only able to take this well-earned breakfast break thanks to the young girls that were up in the street at that moment building the stalls.

This morning, thanks to her now employment of the young wan, Nellie Nugent was able to set foot in the café for breakfast for the first time in years. John Joe O'Reilly spotted Nellie the moment she entered. He knew her face, he knew she was a dealer, and he could tell that she had not been in his café for some years, but he could not recall why. Nellie, on seeing Marion's mother, made her way to a seat and a table beside her. John Joe arrived there at the same time and was by her side.

"Here, you." John Joe spoke to Nellie sternly, pointing his finger.

Nellie's eyebrows raised. "What?" she was surprised and puzzled.

"I don't want any trouble out of you," John Joe warned.

Nellie looked from Mrs. Delany to John Joe. "What are you fucking talking about?" Nellie now stood up again.

"Didn't I bar you from here for causing trouble?" John Joe asked.

"No," Nellie answered sternly.

"Are you sure?"

"I'm positive," Nellie insisted.

John Joe relaxed. "That's all right, then. Now, ladies, what will it be?" He carried on.

CHAPTER TWENTY-TWO

Marion was correct. Agnes was indeed a "natural" street trader. Although she had not been allowed by Nellie to "sell" yet, Agnes ran her end of the stall like a military operation. She kept the area spotless: no empty boxes, cabbage leaves, or rotted fruit near the stall. Before she stacked the stall with it, every bit of fruit was washed, and her apples were shined within an inch of their lives. Nellie gave no compliments, but it was clear that a healthy respect for the young girl was creeping in. Each morning, Nellie would take her tea break about 11:30 and cross the street to have a cup of tea with Mrs. Delany. The tea came from Maher's Pub, at least the boiling water did. The dealers all had their own mugs, teapots, and sugar. The pub would allow them to fill their teapots free of charge from a huge Burko boiler that was kept on the boil all day. Marion and Agnes took turns at fetching and making the tea. When it was prepared, the two older women would sit on apple boxes and the youngsters would work the stalls. Agnes looked forward to this short spell of standing on the platform each day. She would serve to the odd customer, weighing out the fruit and vegetables and always tossing an extra tomato or apple into the bag over the weight. She had noticed Nellie doing this, and the reaction of the customers when they saw that little extra being given to them.

"She's very good, isn't she?" Mrs. Delany remarked to Nellie.

Mrs. Delany had noticed Nellie watching Agnes as the young girl served yet another customer. Nellie sipped on her tea.

"She smiles a lot," Nellie said in reply. "Customers like that." She took another sip. Then she produced a half-smoked cigarette from her coat pocket. The butt was wrinkled and bent. Nellie carefully straightened it out, placed it between her lips, and lit it, never taking her eyes from Agnes across the street.

"When are you going to get her selling?" Mrs. Delany asked.

"I'll see." Nellie wasn't committing herself.

"It's been six months now. I think she could be up to it."

"I said I'll see. Didn't I say that?" Nellie didn't like being pushed. Mrs. Delany backed off.

"Jesus, keep your hair on, I was only making a comment." She began to tidy up the tea things. Time to get back to work.

"My mother didn't let me sell for a year," Nellie stated.

"Maybe you weren't as good as Agnes." Mrs. Delany smirked.

Nellie laughed. "You are a wagon, Delany." They both laughed now. They gathered up the tea things and rinsed out the mugs for the two young wans to use. It would be Marion and Agnes' tea break next.

Nellie threw her cigarette butt on the ground and stood on it. "I wasn't," Nellie said.

"What?" Mrs. Delany asked.

"I wasn't as good as that young wan." Nellie nodded toward Agnes.

Mrs. Delany smiled. "I'll see you later, Nellie." And she went back to her stall.

"Selling" is not a simple as it sounds, and is completely different to *serving*, which is what Agnes was doing during Nellie's tea breaks now. The art of selling, especially in an open-air market, encompassed many individual talents. If you are selling Brussels sprouts, for instance, you are surrounded by women who are also selling them. So you are trying to tell customers to buy from you and not from them. At the same time, you must not offend the other women. So you must cry out your description of the sprouts in a way that gives them a uniqueness, and you must do it in a tone that makes the customer believe that *you* believe they are the best sprouts in the world. So there is a wealth of difference between calling "Brussels sprouts, twopence a pound" and "last of the Brussels sprouts, straight from the royal farms of Luxembourg, just a couple of pounds left." You must not allow facts like there is no royal family in Luxembourg or that you actually have ten stone of them left to cloud the issue. It must be cried with conviction, with style, and whenever possible with comedy. This could be done by holding up a head of cabbage as an example of one of the "royal" sprouts. So it was important that, when a new seller was introduced to the street, she was ready, and that her distinct cry would be an addition to the melody of the street, which attracted tourists just to hear the women sell. Nellie was being careful. That's all.

Agnes loved the street, with a passion. Each morning, she came to work with a smile on her face. She was very organized, and this rubbed off on Marion, whose delighted mother had now increased her wages to three pounds a week. Agnes had also little by little changed the design of the stall. Gone was the traditional pyramid, replaced by the stepped design usually favored by the flower sellers. When racked out, the stall was now one of the most colorful and attractive on the fruit-and-vegetable end of the street. Agnes made the changes gradually over the first year of her working with Nellie. Nellie pretended not to notice the changes and made no comment, except for the apron. The dealers wore smocks over their day clothes. These were little more than glorified dresses, without pockets and shapeless. When it was cold on the street, which was most of the time, they would wear coats or jackets over the smocks. Because there were no pockets in the smocks, money was kept hidden on the stall, in a biscuit or oxo tin. This meant that if a dealer moved away from the stall at all her tin came with her. Into the bathroom they would march, tin under the arm. So Agnes had an idea. Based on what she saw a butcher wearing, she made an apron that went over her head and tied about the waist. She sewed two pockets into the front of the apron, where she could keep her precious key and some odds and ends, lipstick and cigarettes, for Agnes now smoked, and now approaching sixteen, she found makeup becoming very important. The apron was a great success, and Marion gave Agnes the money to buy the fabric and make one for her too. Nellie left it some weeks before commenting on it.

"Where did you get the apron?" she asked one day out of the blue.

"I made it meself," Agnes said with pride.

"Quite the little seamstress, aren't we?" was Nellie's reply, but said with a smile. Even her noticing the apron was a big thing for Nellie. Agnes smiled to herself. That night, she began sewing an apron for Nellie. It took her three nights to finish it, and when Nellie arrived from the wholesalers' the fourth day she discovered the new apron lying folded on the stall.

"Here, young wan," she called. "Your apron is here." She held it up.

"That's not mine, it's yours, Mrs. Nugent. I made it for you," Agnes said matter-of-factly, and carried on unloading the pram.

Nellie was speechless. She looked about her to see if anybody was noticing her embarrassment. Nellie was unused to acts of kindness.

"How much did this cost?" she asked.

"It doesn't matter, Mrs. Nugent. It's a present." Agnes kept working through this exchange.

"I don't want no fuckin' presents. I'll pay me way. How much is it?" Nellie insisted.

But Agnes wasn't backing down. She stopped working and let fly at the woman. "It's a fuckin' present! You can't buy it. If you want to wear it, then wear it; if you don't want to, then throw it in the bin, I don't care." But she did. Agnes went back to work.

Nellie threw the apron back on the stall and went to work herself. Mumbling, but loud enough for Agnes to hear. "You watch your tongue, miss, don't you cheek me. Little bitch. And the fuckin' language out of you." She mumbled on. Agnes ignored her.

Later that day, Marion and Agnes had gone around to the Pillar Café in O'Connell Street for their break, and a very important subject came up. Boys.

"It's all right for you, Agnes. Every boy that walks down Moore Street has his tongue hanging out when he sees you," Marion was moaning. "I could stand up on the stall in me nude with a carrot sticking out of me arse and they'd walk straight past, or ask how much the carrots are." Agnes nearly choked on her cream bun, laughing at the thought of Marion naked on top of the stall. Marion wasn't joking.

"Really, Aggie, you have to come with me to the dance. You get the boys over to us and I'll finish them off; please come, just one night," Marion begged. Marion had taken to going to the dance halls on Friday nights. It was the in thing. She would ask Agnes to go with her every week, but week after week Agnes declined, saying that she had no interest, and could not afford it anyway. With Dolly in her last year at school, Agnes was saving her money to have enough to buy her some clothes to wear for when she went looking for a job.

"Marion, I don't like dances, I'm not going," Agnes insisted.

"How do you know you don't like them? You've never been!" Marion wasn't giving up.

"I'm not going. That's that." Agnes held her hand up to signify the end to the matter. They finished their tea without further mention of the dances. When they returned to work, there was lots to do, and Agnes got stuck into it. As she worked that afternoon, her smile was even broader than usual, for on her return she saw that Nellie Nugent was selling away with great gusto, wearing her new apron.

The following Friday evening, as Agnes was putting away the last of the stall with Marion, Nellie came down to the sheds to pay her. She handed Agnes three pound notes folded, and as Agnes took them she could feel coins in the middle of the fold. Agnes opened the bills to find two half-crowns. Five shillings extra!

"What's this?" Agnes asked. Then she frowned. "Wait a second, if this is for the apron you can stick it!" Agnes was insulted.

Nellie held her hands up. "Will you stop jumping on everything I do, young wan? It's not for that piece of shite that you call an apron. You might have forgot, but you are a year working with me this week. It's a raise, that's all. You're due it. See you on Monday, and don't be late." Nellie left. Agnes was never late, but Nellie said this every Friday. Agnes stood looking after her with the money in her hand.

"A raise?" Marion said as she emerged from the shed. "Now you have no excuse. You're coming dancing, Agnes Reddin!"

CHAPTER TWENTY-THREE

There are many ways for girls to meet boys in Dublin: in school, at the local fish-and-chip shop, around some of the Sunday spots like the Botanic Gardens if you live on the Northside or St. Stephen's Green if you lived on the Southside. But nowhere were you more certain of a "cuirt" than at a dance.

The dance scene in Dublin was divided into two. There were the "hops," impromptu dance nights held by various local clubs or the parish-hall committees. These were in general innocent affairs, well supervised by adults or even priests, and the boys and girls were kept well apart from each other. Hops were generally attended by the younger teenagers, though from time to time the odd hairy teenager popped up. These were usually farm boys from the country areas that skirted Dublin, and rather than a quick squeeze these men were actually looking for a wife.

In the City Centre was the other half of the dance scene. The ballrooms. Now, although the word "ballroom" conjures up thoughts of women in swirling taffeta dresses, elegant men in dinner suits, Dublin's ballrooms were nowhere near these thoughts, and dancing was not their primary function. These were ballrooms of romance. Somewhere to "score." Somewhere to "shift," or get a "wearo," or, even better, a "feel." The rooms themselves were dirty, stuffy places with a pall of blue cigarette smoke hanging permanently in the air, and although only tea and lemonade were usually served, the rooms reeked of the alcohol odor spewing from every male breath. For rarely will a Dublin boy or man venture into the dance before midnight and after a feed of gargle. The dress code was strict, skirts or dresses for women, shirt and tie and jacket or suits for men. No matter that the carpet was sticky and the walls damp with condensation: for Agnes, as she was pulled into the Macushla Ballroom for the first time, it was magic. The place heaved with bodies, the music blared from the stage, the huge crystal ball in the center of the ceiling sent tiny sparkles of light around the room and across the faces of the young men and girls who stood in groups smiling and chatting. Agnes stood there wide-eyed and speechless, expecting at any moment to see Humphrey Bogart or even James Dean cross the gigantic empty dance floor. Empty dance floor?

"Nobody's dancing," Agnes shouted to Marion.

"Whah?"

"I said nobody is dancing," Agnes repeated.

"Of course not, its too early. Come on, let's get a spot at the radiator." Marion began to tug at Agnes.

They moved further into the room and Agnes spotted a small empty table beside a radiator. She halted.

"There's a spot," she screamed, but Marion shook her head.

"No, that's their side," she said, and moved on.

Puzzled, Agnes went after Marion. Marion was now moving through the crowd like a ferret, but Agnes caught up with her.

"Whose side?" Agnes asked.

"Theirs—the fellas—that's their side. Our side's over there." Marion pointed to the wall on the other side of the ballroom. On that other wall there were over three hundred girls standing all alone. No men. Agnes looked back at the opposite wall and was now aware that the crowd that was there, again about another three hundred, were all men. The room was rectangular, so it had two long walls and two short walls. The two end short walls belonged to the couples, boys and girls with steady girlfriends and boyfriends. The goal of every person on the long walls was to eventually move to one of the short walls. At a screaming level, Marion explained all of this to Agnes. Agnes realized that she had much to learn about going to a dance.

"How do we meet the boys, if they're over there and we're over here?" she asked Marion.

"I'll tell you in a minute," Marion answered. "Let's get a spot first."

Agnes was puzzled and was about to be stunned, for whereas Agnes was trying to help by looking out for a place on the wall that was unoccupied, Marion was just looking for a "good" spot. When she found the spot she was looking for, Marion pointed it out to Agnes. "There, over there," she called, and went for it. There were already four girls around this radiator, but no matter, Marion barged over, and Agnes watched the exchange open-mouthed.

"Who are you?" Marion asked the biggest of the four girls.

"Joan McCarthy," the girl answered.

"From where?" Marion was like a detective.

The girl glanced to her friends and got no support. "Mountjoy Square," the girl answered.

Marion pointed at the wall behind the girls. They all turned to see, just above the radiator, the words etched in the plaster, "The Jarro." The girls turned back to Marion, the big girl now taking up the cause. "So what?" the big girl asked.

Marion leaned closer to the big girl. "So move," Marion said threateningly.

"Look, we just came here to dance," the big girl stated a bit dismissively.

Marion did not blink. "You won't get many dances with a fuckin' broken leg, love," she answered, and the four girls promptly moved.

The evening was great fun. Agnes hadn't a clue how to dance, so refused the forty or so requests she had from boys and men of all shapes and sizes. She was content just to soak up the magic and the atmosphere. Marion, on the other hand, was a super little dancer, and received no requests. So Marion danced with other girls. This was not unusual; in fact, the first hour of dancing was done by the girls only.

"Come on and dance with me, Agnes," Marion roared over the music to Agnes.

"No. I can't dance, Marion!" Agnes shook her head, which was beginning to get a little fuzzy, as Marion had introduced Agnes to Mr. Smirnoff and Mr. Coca-Cola.

"I'll teach you, come on," Marion insisted.

Agnes scanned the dance floor. The music that was playing was "How Much Is That Doggie in the Window?" And the floor was moving in a clockwise parade of waltzers, most of them girls with girls. Agnes thought they looked silly. She shook her head. "No, Marion. Not yet, maybe in a couple of weeks, but not yet." She really did not want to try it.

At the end of the waltz, the master of ceremonies made an announcement. "Ladies and gentlemen, boys and girls, here's the latest from America. By Bill Haley and the Comets." And it started. Even before the music began, the girls ran screaming onto the dance floor. They paired off with each other and waited, the energy filling the room.

"One, two, three o'clock, four o'clock, rock" boomed out from the Tannoy, and the rest of the song was sung in unison by the crowd. The dance floor looked as if it had been invaded by a herd of whirling dervishes as the heaving mass began to "jive."

Agnes was enthralled. She didn't know what the feeling was, but her foot began to tap, her head to shake, and she wanted to dive onto the floor and go crazy. Agnes was witnessing the birth of "rock and roll."

"Oh Jesus, Marion, I have to learn that!" she screamed at her tiny friend.

"Come on, then," roared Marion, and extended her hand.

"Not now. Not here. But you have to teach me," Agnes pleaded.

Over the next week, Agnes jived around her flat, herself and Marion providing the song, breathlessly singing as they danced. Agnes took to it well, too well for Marion's liking. Marion would finish each session with her nylons twisted around her ankles and thankful that she still had her knickers on. Connie sat bemused, watching tiny Marion trying to throw Agnes over her shoulder; Connie hadn't a clue what was going on, but she smiled and even clapped along at times. By the following week, Agnes could jive, and even Dolly knew the words of the song by heart. Rock and roll had invaded the Jarro. The following Friday night, Agnes took a dance from the first boy that asked her, and from then on there was no shortage of boys looking to dance, so Agnes jived the night away. She loved rock and roll, she loved dancing. She was hooked. The thrill of her first night on the tiles was, however, about to be overshadowed.

On her return home to her flat at midnight, she found her mother, who was supposed to be in the care of Dolly, sitting outside the flat, on the landing, chilled to the bone. Agnes took the cold and confused woman into her bed and covered her up. There was no sign of Dolly.

"Mammy, where's Dolly?" she asked her mother gently.

"Gone. She's gone," Connie said.

"Gone where, Mammy? Please, it's important!" Agnes was furious with Dolly but didn't show it to her mother.

"The police took her away, they came and took her," Connie said as she drifted away.

CHAPTER TWENTY-FOUR

Store Street Police Station was packed. Friday night was a busy one for the Gardai. Black Marias were lining up to spew out the scum of the night into the station. Agnes made her way past groping drunks and screaming derelicts to the reception area. There was a young policeman manning the desk. As Agnes approached, he was writing in a huge book.

"Excuse me, please," Agnes called to him over the din.

He didn't look up from his work. "What?" he asked the book.

"I'm trying to find my sister," she said.

The young officer looked up. As was usual, Agnes was pretty enough to get his full attention. He smiled. "Well, if she's anything as pretty as you, we should have no problem finding her." He opened his book again and prepared to take notes. "Now, when did you see her last?" he asked.

Agnes cut to the chase. "She's here. Well, I think she is."

"Here?" The Garda looked up slowly. "What is she doing here?" He was not as interested in Agnes now.

"I don't know."

"What's the name?" He lifted the charge roster.

"Reddin. Dolly Reddin." Agnes tried to read the list upside down, but couldn't. The young Garda ran his finger down the list. Then stopped.

"She's here all right. She's a burglar, then?"

"What? Burglar? Oh Christ, I'll kill her!" Agnes began to sob. "Can I see her?" she asked.

Dolly looked so scared, sitting in the interview room alone. Agnes looked in at her through the wired glass window in the door. Dolly's eyes were red from crying, and she was shaking.

"Five minutes. You can see her in the morning, then, in court. She's up at ten-thirty a.m.," the policeman said. Then he opened the door. When she entered, Dolly ran to her and threw her arms about her.

"Oh, Agnes, I'm afraid."

Dolly was shocked when Agnes pushed her away. "You little bitch! How could you?" Agnes screamed. "Leaving Mammy alone is bad enough, but back to your old tricks with your scumbag friends!" Agnes was furious.

"I didn't do anything!" Dolly protested.

But Agnes slapped her across the face. "Don't lie to me!"

Dolly began to cry softly. She sat back down in the chair and just stared at the floor, rocking back and forth. Agnes knocked on the door to be let out of the room.

"I knew you wouldn't believe me," Dolly said to her older sister's back. Agnes left. She cried all the way home.

Nellie Nugent did not ask, but she could tell that there was something wrong with Agnes. When Nellie arrived at the stall with the pram full of produce, Agnes had virtually dumped it onto the stall, rather than her usual placing of each different item like a sculptor. She let her work on. If Agnes had something to say, Nellie was certain she would say it when she needed to.

Nellie got her result at about 9 a.m. Agnes approached her nervously.

"Mrs. Nugent, can I take some of the morning off?" she asked.

"For what?" Nellie asked, sending Agnes into a flood of tears. Nellie got a start at this reaction. She went to Agnes and held her by the shoulders.

"Christ Almighty, what's wrong, child?" she asked. Agnes wriggled out of Nellie's grip, but instead of pulling away, she put her arms around the big woman's waist and buried her head in Nellie's huge bosom. Nellie was startled by this and didn't know what to do. She stood there with Agnes gripping on to her, and she with her arms wide like a Christ on the crucifix.

"Pull yourself together, young wan!" Nellie admonished her. But Agnes just cried. Slowly Nellie closed her arms and hugged the young girl. Then she began to pat the child on the back, saying, "There, there, there." Agnes calmed. Nellie's voice and the patting of her back made her feel protected. Agnes would learn to do this to calm anyone she had crying in her own arms for the rest of her life. When she was calm, Nellie sat Agnes down and made her tell the whole story.

When she had finished the telling, Nellie asked, "What makes you think that she did do anything?"

Agnes was aghast at the question. "She's on probation, she's done it before, and anyway the police don't make that kind of mistake."

Nellie raised an eyebrow at this last part. "Yes, they do," she asserted. "And right now what your sister needs more than anything is for *you* to believe her."

"Do you think they could be wrong, really?" Agnes asked.

"The chances of somebody being innocent increase in direct proportion to the amount of people trying to prove them guilty," Nellie recited the longest sentence Agnes had ever heard her utter. Agnes hadn't a clue what she was talking about. It showed in her face. Nellie thought of explaining, then changed her mind. "What time is the court case?" she asked.

"Half past ten. Do you mind if I go?" Agnes asked.

"I'll get Mrs. Delany to mind our stall. We'll both go down there." Nellie stood. She ran her hand over Agnes' head and went across the street to make the arrangements. The use of the phrase "our stall" was not lost on Agnes.

The children's court was packed. It was half an hour before Dolly was ushered in from the holding room. Agnes and Nellie were about halfway down the stuffed courtroom.

"Dolly!" Agnes cried to her sister. Dolly looked around but did not see her. Agnes began to push her way to the front of the room, all the while calling Dolly's name. She fell and still did not stop, crawling now on her hands and knees. She moved between legs, and when she saw a gap she made for it and stood, calling loudly, "DOLLY!" Where she stood she was just two feet from her sister. Dolly looked terrible. She looked Agnes in the eyes.

"I'm sorry, Agnes," she said softly.

"No. I'm sorry, Dolly. I believe you, I do, I believe you!" Agnes cried.

"Really?"

"Really! I believe you!" They made to hug, but Dolly was tugged away to stand before the judge.

What followed was wrong, all wrong. Not just wrong in the moral sense but incorrect. Dolly was charged with a burglary that took place at 10:15 p.m. the previous Wednesday. The police had caught two girls, and those girls had given the names of three other girls that they said were involved. Dolly's name was on that list.

"It couldn't have been her," Agnes called from the courtroom floor. The judge asked who had spoken, and Agnes raised her hand.

"It couldn't have been Dolly; she was with me. My friend was teaching me to dance, and Dolly was there, with us." Agnes was thrilled. Nellie was right, policemen do make mistakes.

"And who are you?" the judge asked Agnes.

"I'm Agnes Reddin. I'm her sister," Agnes stated proudly. Agnes was about to discover that not only do policemen make mistakes, so do judges.

"Her sister? Her sister? Well, that evidence is about as reliable as a cardboard boat in a storm!" This drew a laugh from the policemen and lawyers gathered in the room.

Nellie spoke up. "The other girl is a witness too. Marion, Marion Delany," she called out.

Agnes turned and mouthed "Thanks" to her, then turned to the judge. "I'll go and get Marion. She can be here in ten minutes!" Agnes promised. The judge was not impressed.

"If you think now that I am going to hold up the proceedings of this court just so as you can go and get one of your guttersnipe friends to lie for you, you have another think coming! Any previous?" He turned to the Garda.

"She's on probation, Your Honor, three years," the Garda offered.

"For what?" the judge asked.

"Burglary," the Garda said.

"Aha!" the judge exclaimed. "I knew it! Well, now, I'm the man to teach you a lesson!" He put on some reading glasses and began writing, then pronounced sentence. "Young lady, you are to be placed into an institution of the state at the pleasure of the Minister for Justice." He banged his gavel. "Next," he called, and Dolly was taken away.

Nellie was finding it difficult to explain "the Minister's Pleasure" to Agnes.

"Until she is eighteen, is it?" Agnes asked. Nellie shook her head.

"Could be shorter, or longer. Her case will come up for review every so often. If the Minister is having a good day she could be out," Nellie explained.

"And if he is having a bad day?" Agnes asked.

Nellie shrugged. "Who knows?"

"But she's only *thirteen!*" Agnes began to sob loudly.

Nellie hugged her. "There, there, there," she whispered, as she brushed her hand over Agnes' dark mane.

CHAPTER TWENTY-FIVE

Dolly was incarcerated in St. Mary's Home for Delinquent Girls, in Oldgrange, just outside Dublin. It was two hours by bus each way to visit, and Agnes was allowed just half an hour with her sister per week. In the six months since Dolly had been placed there, Agnes did not miss one Sunday. Marion would accompany Agnes on the bus trip, but would not be allowed to visit Dolly. It pained Agnes to watch Dolly deteriorate. She was getting a hard time in there, but refused to waste any of the half-hour they had together talking about it.

This was to change a little for the better, though, after a chat with Nellie on Monday. Agnes and Nellie were working the stall, and there was a lull in the business.

"How's your sister getting on?" Nellie asked. Agnes told Nellie how Dolly was looking awful and how worried she was about her. Nellie listened and told Agnes not to worry, that her sister would settle down. It didn't work. Agnes was still worried.

"Jesus, I think I'll head off early, young wan, I'm not feeling the best." Nellie did not look the best either. She had been sick for some time but refused to attend a doctor. "Don't bother me, young wan, with those fuckin' quacks!" is all Nellie would say each time Agnes suggested it.

"Do you want me to finish the day?" Agnes asked.

"No. Just wrap up the stall." Nellie was putting her coat on. She still had not let Agnes sell. Even after three years. Agnes didn't show her disappointment. She wrapped the stall and, as it was only one o'clock in the afternoon, joined Marion at her stall for the rest of the day.

The following Sunday, Agnes was stopped at the gate of St. Mary's on her way in to visit Dolly.

"Where are you going?" the guard asked.

"To visit my sister, Dolly Reddin!" Agnes was puzzled. She had never been stopped before.

"Wait here," the guard said, and retreated to his little hut. Agnes looked to Marion, who shrugged. Agnes now began to worry. Was there something wrong with Dolly? Had she been hurt? By the time the guard returned, all kinds of scenarios were going through her head.

"It's supposed to be just one visitor a week. Your mother was here on Monday. I'll let you off with it this time, but don't let it happen again." He opened the gate, but Agnes didn't move.

"My mother? She was here?" Agnes was dazed. The man looked at his clipboard.

"Constance Reddin? Is that your mother?" he asked.

"Yes. That's her."

"Then she was here. Now go on before I change me mind." Agnes rushed in. As she walked to the visitors' room she was numb. Her mother didn't even know that Dolly was here! How could it be? The answer was waiting for her in the visitors' room.

"Nellie Nugent? She came to see you?" Agnes was incredulous. A much-better-looking Dolly nodded her head.

"Why? What did she say?" Agnes asked.

"A lot," Dolly answered, and recounted the visit to Agnes. Nellie had taken the half-hour with Dolly to tell her about some of her experiences in prison. She went over with Dolly some tips for keeping herself right. And, most important of all, she had given Dolly a note to give to a girl in there named Barbara Brady, an acquaintance of Nellie's. Barbara Brady, Dolly explained, was the toughest, hardest girl in there. The note told Barbara that she should look after Dolly or answer to Nellie when she got out. Since Monday last, Dolly's life in there had become so much easier.

"I've joined the library in here, and I'm enrolling for bookkeeping classes," Dolly announced. Agnes was so relieved to see Dolly relaxed and even smiling. She left that day in better form than she had been in for weeks.

Friday night, Agnes and Marion went dancing for the first time since the night of Dolly's arrest. Yet again Agnes was surrounded by boys wanting to jive with her, while as usual Marion was still dancing with girls.

When she returned to work the following Monday, Agnes tried to thank Nellie. When Nellie arrived from the wholesalers', Agnes went to her immediately. "Mrs. Nugent, I can't thank you enough for going to see Dolly." She smiled. Nellie didn't.

"Well, I had to do something. This stall has gone to shit, and your work is terrible, I'd be better off on me own!" She refused to be thanked.

"I'll do better, I promise I will."

"Yeh better, I can get another young wan anytime, so mind your job!" Nellie finished, and went to work. They never spoke of her visit to Dolly again.

"Here," Nellie called to Agnes when she had the stall packed, "you go on and have a break."

Agnes made her way over to Marion's stall. As she approached the stall, she noticed that Marion was reading something. Her eyes were squinting.

"What's that?" Agnes asked Marion.

"Tickets," Marion answered, and put the tickets into her apron pocket. This was quite a deliberate move on Marion's part, for she knew it would arouse Agnes' interest.

"Tickets? Tickets for what?" Agnes asked with a tone that denoted her belief that she had a right to know, and now.

"Tickets to a dance . . . Ah, you wouldn't be interested." Marion feigned a lack of interest.

"What dance?" Of course Agnes was interested.

Marion stared at Agnes for a few moments, pretending defiance, but then just as easily she pretended surrender. "Okay, well, if you must know, it's a dance on Tuesday night to raise funds for a charity." Marion began to busy herself on the stall and walked to the far side of it. Agnes followed her around the stall.

"And?" Agnes waited.

"And what?" Marion answered.

"Are we going?" Agnes groaned.

"Well, I might. You can if you want to."

"Where is it?"

"In St. Martin's School Hall." Marion threw the name out like it was nothing.

Agnes' mug froze on the way to her mouth. Her brow furrowed, puzzled. "The fuckin' deaf school?"

"Yep." Marion carried on.

"Ah, Marion, you're jokin' me—a dance for deaf people."

"I'm not joking you, and why shouldn't deaf people dance?"

"To what? What are they going to dance to?"

"The music," said Marion as if it were a stupid question.

"They can't hear the fuckin' music, Marion; don't be stupid."

"Well, Miss Know-It-All, for your information they can—well, in a different way they can. What they do is, the band put the speakers onto the dance floor and keep the music real loud, and the deaf people dance to the vibration," Marion explained. Agnes was aghast now that she realized Marion was serious.

"Marion Delany, you are getting desperate for a man."

"I am not."

"You are."

"Not."

"Are."

"Not."

"Are."

"Agnes!!!" came the scream from Nellie Nugent across the street.

"Oh, shite." Agnes threw her cigarette on the ground and stood on it. "I'll see you later; this one's like a whore on a Honda today." Agnes scurried away. As she left, Marion called after her, "Not."

Nellie Nugent was not happy as usual. "I said take a break, not a fuckin' holiday," she barked at Agnes.

"Sorry, Mrs. Nugent," Agnes apologized.

"Now, start screaming there and sell a few of these carrots before they go black," Nellie ordered.

Agnes was stunned. Nellie was telling her to "sell." She stood frozen for a moment, unsure that she had heard correctly.

"What are you waiting for?" Nellie goaded her. Agnes had waited for this moment since the day she first came onto the street. But she'd thought she would get some warning, a day's notice or something. Agnes picked up a bunch of carrots.

"How much, Mrs. Nugent?" Agnes asked softly.

"Truppence a pound," Nellie announced.

Agnes nodded and moved to the street side of the stall. She cleared her throat and began. "Nice carrots truppence a pound," called Agnes, but her voice was just a gentle mumble, like a hymn. "Nice carrots truppence a pound," she sang again.

Nellie Nugent slowly looked up from her racking out of the stall, her mouth open in a stunned expression. Some other dealers began to notice, and they stopped calling out. Now the shoppers noticed that nobody was calling, and they stopped in their tracks and looked around to see what the dealers were looking at. The Henry Street end of Moore Street was now silent, except for Agnes' little voice.

"Nice carrots, truppence a pound." They all stared in wonder at her as she again gently sang, "Nice carrots, truppence a pound."

For the first time, the traders listened to her little song. It was a shopper that laughed first, followed by some of the stall holders, but it eventually built into a roar of laughter. Agnes stopped and blushed. Nellie Nugent stepped off her box and walked onto the street to Agnes. Nellie stood with her face just inches from Agnes' face. Agnes was now so embarrassed that her eyes began to fill. She wanted to throw herself into Nellie's big bosom and bury her face again. Nellie opened her mouth, and the loudest scream Agnes ever heard came out. "NICE CARROTS, TRUPPENCE A POUND," she yelled.

Agnes' hair blew back from her face with the power of Nellie's voice. Her embarrassment deepened, and a tear ran down her face. Marion, who had been laughing, now stopped, and her heart sank as she watched Agnes crumble before Nellie.

"Sing it out, girlie! You are SELLING, not BEGGING!" Nellie told Agnes and the rest of the street.

Agnes' lips trembled; she turned and ran through the crowd. Marion took off her apron, threw it on the stall, and followed after Agnes. In the distance she saw Agnes slip into the door of Madigan's Pub. When Marion entered Madigan's, she first looked into the snug. It was empty. She made for the toilets. As soon as Marion pushed the door of the toilet open, she could hear the sobbing. Agnes had locked herself into one of the three cubicles, so Marion leaned against the door and knocked gently.

"Are you okay, Aggie?" she asked softly.

There was no reply.

"Aggie, are you all right?" Marion asked again.

"Go away," Agnes answered after a moment.

Marion took a cigarette from her pocket and scratched a match down the wall of the toilet. The sulfur ignited, and Marion put it to the end of the cigarette. She took a slow drag and let the smoke flow from her mouth, watching it spiral upward to the light from the only window in the toilets. She blew out the match and leaned back against the wall. When Marion spoke, she spoke to the smoke. "I remember my first time to call on the street. I was standing by my mother at the stall one day and she just said to me, 'Get out there and do a bit of selling, you.' I looked across the stall. Me ma had lots of stuff, but the stuff that caught my eye was the grapes shining in the sun and little wooden boxes of dates—they used to come in wooden boxes, you know, eight to a box. So I takes a box of dates and stands on me mother's crate and starts screaming: '*Black grapes, green grapes, dried dates, a shilling for eight.*' Jesus, it sounds easy now, but when I was screaming it was coming out '*Blackgreatgreengreat-drieddrateshillingfree.*'" Marion laughed alone; no sound came from the cubicle. "I swear to God there was people thought I was fuckin' Albanian. Me mother grabbed me with her hand over me mouth like she was kidnapping me and dragged me to the back of the stall. 'Here,' says she, 'don't try and sell everything in one breath.' 'Why?' says I. 'What do you want me to do?' 'Pick the best thing on the stalls,' says she, 'and sell that, and when the customer sees what else you've got she'll buy some of that as well.' 'Right,' says I. Then I asked her, 'Well, what's the best thing on our stall, Ma?' 'You are,' says she, and she winked at me. I had to think about that for a minute, but then I got it. So I got up on the box and I picked an aul one out who was just walking by. 'Missus,' says I, 'come over here and let me look after you, you look like you're lost or something.' Your one smiled at me and came over. Two boxes of dates I sold her, and a bunch of mixed herbs. I'll never forget it. I've been watching me mother selling all her life, and the first time I tried it I made a balls of it. Aggie, if you're listening, I don't know how you're going to get paid enough money to go to Canada, but you won't find it in there." Marion tossed her cigarette end into the toilet bowl; it hissed as it hit the water. She flushed the toilet and left.

When Marion arrived back at her stall, her mother asked, "Is your friend all right?"

Marion nodded and began selling again. "Beautiful Cox's pippins, penny each, seven for a tenner. Jesus, missus, that's a lovely coat, he must really love you , would you not bring him home a few Coxes?" She winked at a customer.

Nellie Nugent had seen Agnes coming back long before the young girl had reached the stall, but she pretended not to until Agnes stood across the stall from her. Nellie looked into Agnes' face; the girl had been crying.

"What?" Nellie asked Agnes impatiently.

"Still carrots?" Agnes asked.

"Still carrots, and still fuckin' truppence," Nellie answered and began serving an elderly woman.

Agnes bent and rummaged under the canvas cover of the stall, eventually pulling out a wooden crate. She dragged it a couple of feet from the stall.

Marion, on the far side of the street, was nudged by her mother as she was weighing out some mushrooms for a customer. "Look," her mother said with a nod in Agnes' direction. Marion stopped and watched.

Agnes stood up on the crate and held a handful of carrots in the air. She took a deep breath. "Beautiful golden carrots, pulled first thing this morning, only truppence a pound!" Her voice sailed across the crowded street.

"Fresh carrots, truppence a pound!" Now her voice took on a songlike lilt. "Beeoootiful Irish carrots, treeepence a pow-end," she called, now in a melodious song. A woman tugged at Agnes' skirt.

"I'll take two pound of those, love, please," the woman asked.

Nellie answered before Agnes could. "Here, love! I'll serve you, she's busy *selling*. Keep it going, Agnes love." Nellie began to weigh out the carrots. Agnes continued to sing. She looked over at Marion. They shared a smile.

Marion's customer prompted her. "Are you all right, love? I'm waiting for me mushrooms."

"Give me a minute, missus, I'm not a fuckin' machine," Marion snapped as she poured the mushrooms into a bag.

"She'll be all right," Marion's mother declared, assessing Agnes.

"Yeh, Mammy. She will, she'll be all right," Marion answered.

On that day, the Moore Street melody added another voice to its chorus.

CHAPTER TWENTY-SIX

From that day onward, the relationship between Agnes and Nellie Nugent blossomed. Nellie began to give Agnes more and more responsibility, and Agnes took to being a "selling" dealer with great gusto and a hunger to learn more and more about the trade. And for learning about the trade she couldn't have been working with anyone better than Nellie Nugent.

Nellie began to take Agnes to the wholesalers', showing her how to buy. This was important, she would emphasize to Agnes. "Being a good stall trader is not about how good you sell, it's about how good you buy." She would point things out to Agnes that Agnes wouldn't have dreamed of looking at. For instance, when buying potatoes, track where the potatoes came from. Always buy potatoes that were grown near coastal areas rather than in the Midlands. The reason for this was that the coastal-area land was much sandier and thus there would be less muck on the potatoes. That meant more potatoes per four-stone bag. She would even have Agnes checking every bag of potatoes for stones. Every time they would go to weigh out potatoes for a customer and find a stone in it, they would keep it to one side. Then, once every fortnight, Nellie would bring a huge bag of stones down to the wholesalers and say, "These are not potatoes; give me back my money." The wholesalers rarely argued. They would just simply stick the stones on the scales and pay her back, pound for pound.

If Agnes had gone looking for a mentor, she couldn't have found a better one. And not just that—she had also found herself a very strong mother figure, and she needed it, for at home things were getting worse and worse.

Agnes' mother, Connie, had virtually vanished into a cocoon from which she emerged very seldom and for only brief periods. So, on top of the hard work and learning that Agnes was going through, learning the tricks of the trade down in Moore Street, the rest of her day would be spent washing and cleaning the house, pandering to her mother's needs, paying the bills, and keeping the wolf from the door. She entertained herself one night a week only, Friday, when she would go dancing with Marion and a gang of the young wans from the markets. This was her night of pleasure. Her dancing had so improved that Marion was suggesting Agnes should enter into competitions. Agnes sunned the idea, for it usually meant that one had a permanent partner, and Agnes hadn't time for a boy-friend. Mind you, this last week she had taken a couple of kisses from the odd partner, and she even made a date—with a soldier, no less. She didn't mention this to Nellie, as *her* track record with sol-diers was not good.

Dolly had settled into prison well. Agnes kept her promise and visited her every Sunday, taking away her dirty washing and giving her fresh underwear. It was exhausting, though. A typical day for Agnes was to rise at 3:30 a.m., wash, and make her way down to Moore Street. Which was about an hour and a half before Marion arrived. They had come to an arrangement. Agnes now had the key to Marion's mother's shed also, so she would drag the makings of the stalls from both sheds and build the framework, leaving the base and the apple boxes for both stalls built and ready for Marion. Agnes would then head down to the fruit-and-vegetable whole-salers', where she would meet with Nellie. Together they would make the choice of the day's produce for sale, and when this was completed Nellie went for her breakfast to Rosie's and Agnes would head back to her flat. When she got back to the flat, Agnes would raise her mother from bed. She would wash her, dress her, and sit her at the kitchen table. She would cook a breakfast for both of them and have breakfast with her mother. Even though Agnes' mother rarely responded, Agnes carried on conversations with her mother as if she were taking in every word. When they finished the breakfast, Agnes would clean the dishes and leave them on the draining board and then take her mother for a walk to the shops. Connie was well known and liked in the shopping area, so Agnes would leave her there and she would potter from shop to shop, chatting away idly. In the area, most people knew of Connie's dementia, and indeed, on the rare occasions when Connie did come out of her cocoon and talk in the present tense, it would be mostly with these people in the shops, whom she had seen all her life. Agnes, in the meanwhile, would now make her way back to Moore Street, where she would start racking up the stock with Nellie and be ready for the arrival of the horse and cart. With the stall racked out and everything ready to go, Agnes and Marion would sit on an apple box and have their cup of tea. Agnes looked forward to this, as Marion always had something to say, a story to tell, and rarely did these moments pass without Agnes' laughing. The early morning at the stall was its busiest time, so Agnes would split her time between serving and selling. By midday, when things had calmed down a little, Nellie would pop off to Maher's Pub for a bite of lunch. When Nellie returned, Agnes would then leave, heading back up to the shops to collect her mother and take her back to the flat. There she would cook a lunch for both of them and put her mother down for a nap before returning to the stall in Moore Street. By 3:30 p.m., things would start to wind down, and Agnes would begin to separate any excess stock that had gone off, to dump. Then, leaving all her boxes and rubbish ready for Jacko the box collector in a huge pile, she'd have a cigarette with Marion. Anything that could be saved for the following day would be put into a fresh box and brought down to the shed. Nellie would then say her good nights very briefly and head home for the rest of the day. Agnes would dismantle the stalls and pack them away for the night, returning home just in time to make dinner for her mother. By 7:30 p.m., Agnes was in bed and asleep. Absolutely exhausted. So, needless to say, although it had seemed like a good idea at the time, she now was sorry she had agreed to date the soldier.

On the night of the date, as agreed, Agnes was waiting beneath the huge clock outside Clery's store. He arrived on time and suggested that they take in a movie, and he produced two tickets for the Metropole to see *From Here to Eternity*. Agnes hadn't the heart to tell the chap that she had already seen the movie three times. Nor could she remember his name, so she didn't ask him. When they were seated comfortably in the balcony seats, he put his arm around her. She squirmed out of it. They sat watching the adverts.

"Would you like some popcorn?" he asked.

"I'd love some!" Agnes lied. So the chap left to fetch his date some popcorn. The next thing Agnes knew, she was being shaken and someone was shining a torch in her face.

"Are you all right there? Come on, we are locking up." Agnes looked around. The cinema was empty. Beside her on the empty seat was an untouched bag of popcorn. She had fallen asleep. She never saw the soldier again.

Agnes was loading her pram with the makings of Nellie's stall when Marion arrived the next morning.

"Morning, sleepyhead," called Agnes up the lane.

"Morning, Agnes. How did your date go with the soldier?" Marion asked.

"Don't talk to me, a fucking disaster," Agnes answered.

"Couldn't have been worse than mine," Marion replied, waving off Agnes' moaning.

"It was," Agnes insisted.

"Couldn't have been." Marion was equally insistent.

So Agnes began to recount the events of the previous evening to Marion. Her story went on all through the building of the stalls, and by the time Agnes had finished the telling, the stalls were ready for racking and the girls had drawn two cups of tea from the boiler in Maher's Pub. Throughout Agnes' story Marion had laughed and been shocked in all the right places, and they now sat with their tea and crates beside the empty stalls. Before Agnes lit her cigarette she said, "Now, don't tell me your night was worse than that."

"Well, as bad as that." Marion backed up a little.

"I warned you about going to that dance," Agnes admonished Marion. "So go on, what happened?"

"Well, when I got there the place looked all right. The music was loud—now, I mean really loud. I got myself a drink, and I stood near the bar watching. You should see them deaf and dumb people doing the sign language, it's amazing. Hands flying in all directions. I watched for a bit, and I seen how they say hello, it's kinda like this." Marion lifted up her hand opened and closed it. "So, anyway, I'm standing there for about three or four songs; the next thing, I see this fella; now, he's a beauty, and he comes walking towards me. Then I realize that he's not coming towards me, he's coming *to* me. So I give him the sign for 'hello' and he gives it to me back. Then he points to me and back to himself and wiggles his hips."

"He wanted to dance with you," Agnes interpreted.

"Exactly. So we goes onto the dance floor, and, Jesus, he's a great dancer."

"Sounds great so far." Agnes is getting excited for Marion.

"But wait." Marion holds up her hand.

"Oh, sorry, go on." Agnes sips her tea.

"While we're dancing he taps me and does a sign like this." Marion now points to her eye and puts her arm over her shoulder and pats her own back and then mimes riding a horse.

"I . . . back . . . horses." Agnes shouts out the last word as if she is in a quiz. "He backs horses. He's a gambler?" Agnes asks.

"Is right," says Marion.

"Jesus, it is good, this sign language," Agnes comments.

"But wait." Marion snaps with the hand up again.

"Go on," says Agnes.

"So I nodded, letting him know I understand, and he nods back. Well, I decided to have a go." Marion now stands and points to her eye and then mouths the word "like" and points to her feet. Agnes interprets. "I . . . lick . . . shoes. What the fuck does that mean?"

"I like walking," Marion corrects. "Look at me mouth." Marion mouths the word "like" again. Agnes looks closer. Marion mouths the word "like" again.

"Nah, still looks like 'lick' to me," Agnes says.

"Shut up. Well, he understood," Marion asserted.

"Right. Well, go on—it sounds to me like you were on your way," Agnes encouraged.

"But wait." The hand again.

"Go on, then. But hurry, Nellie will be here any minute. She'll go mad if she just sees us sitting here, and I won't hear the end of this bleedin' story."

"All right. So, anyway, all night we're doing this. He goes to the bar, buys me drink, I'm having a great time. Then he uses the signs to ask me can he walk me home."

"What signs did he use?" Agnes asks.

"Doesn't matter," Marion answers with the hand up again. "I says 'yes,' and when the dance ends and the band are playing the National Anthem I slipped into the ladies'. Well, I came out, right, and he's standing with his back to me with another fella. 'I'm going to a party,' says the stranger to him. 'Would you like to come?' he asks my fella. 'No,' says my fella, 'I can't, I'm stuck with a fuckin' deaf one in the ladies'." Agnes squealed and screamed with laughter.

"It's not funny," Marion says sternly. Agnes continues to laugh. After a few moments Marion is smiling. "Agnes, stop it, really, it's not funny." Marion's smile turns to a laugh, and she now joins Agnes in hysterics. They could not finish their tea, for every time the laughter stopped and they would make to take a sip from the cup the laughter began all over again, harder than the previous time.

"Oh, Marion Delany." Agnes was gasping for breath. "What are we like? Neither of us will ever get a man," she cried, but she was soon to be proved wrong.

CHAPTER TWENTY-SEVEN

It was Friday night. Of course this meant dance night. As pre-arranged, the girls all met in Madigan's Pub. The rule in Madi-gan's Pub is that women will only be served in the snug. Now, although the snug takes up just one-quarter of the area of the pub, half of the customers, the women, were squeezed into it. As usual, Marion was late. Agnes sat at the table with Nine Warts Philomena and Giddy Eye, and they had kept a spare seat for Marion, in front of which stood a bottle of Guinness and a glass on the table ready for her when she arrived. By the time Marion arrived, the snug was crowded with young girls in their dance frocks and their hair that was lacquered into sculptures. Marion spied the gang as soon as she entered and hurried through the crowd to the table.

"Sorry I'm late." Marion was breathless. "I had to do me ma's feet."

"You're all right, Marion, here." Agnes pushed the bottle of Guinness over to Marion.

"I swear to Jaysus, my mammy's toenails grow like bamboos. Look at this one." Marion held up a dark-gray nail clipping that re-sembled a mud flap from a motorbike.

"Ah Jesus," the others cried in unison.

"Marion, for fuck's sake, throw that away," Agnes groaned.

"It's big, but isn't it?" Marion proffered it to Agnes.

"Marion," Agnes screeched.

"It's all right. For God's sake, you think you'd never seen a nail before." Marion dropped the nail clipping into the ashtray. Again the girls spoke in unison: "Not in the ashtray," they cried. Marion picked the nail clipping out and looked around and decided to just toss it over the partition that surrounded the snug. Marion raised her glass and made a toast: "Here's to Friday night, I hope I get a hand on me muff." The girls squealed with laughter, and they all touched glasses and took a drink. Marion wiped her mouth before she spoke. "So—where are we going, the National or the Macushla?"

"I'm barred from the National," said Giddy Eye, seemingly to the light fitting on the ceiling. The girls looked up briefly.

"Since when?" asked Agnes.

"Last Saturday night," replies Giddy Eye, this time to the ashtray. The girls all looked at the ashtray.

"Jesus, barred? For what?" asked Nine Warts Philomena.

"The bouncer said I told him to fuck off. I wasn't even talking to him." Giddy Eye's adrenaline was pumping now with the telling of her story, and the eye was darting in every direction.

"Jaysus, Giddy, I wish you'd wear a patch over that eye, I do be exhausted just trying to listen to you," Marion sighed.

"Ah, fuck off, you," Giddy Eye replied. A woman at the next table butted in, "Fuck off yourself."

"She wasn't talking to you," explained Agnes, then, turning back to the girls, she announced, "Right, then, it's the Macushla. I hope that weirdo isn't there again," Agnes added as an afterthought.

"What weirdo?" Philomena wanted to know. Marion took up the story.

"He's not a weirdo, it's Tommo Monks the coalman."

"Oh, him." Philomena knew him. Tommo Monks delivered coal to Philomena's house every Monday.

Marion went on: "Every time we go to the Macushla, he does be standing across the floor just staring over at Agnes. She thinks he's a weirdo."

"He is," said Agnes.

"He's not," Marion argued. "Maybe he's just shy and he's working up to asking you to dance."

"Oh Jesus, I hope not. I hate saying no to a fella; it's horrible, isn't it?"

Now, Agnes had meant the question for general reception, but she was looking at Philomena when the question ended. Philomena retorted, "What are you fucking asking me for?" Philomena had never said no to a man in her life. In the ballrooms, the men would very unkindly refer to a less-than-beautiful girl as a "bagger." This meant you could make love to this girl provided she wore a bag over her head. Philomena, who was not blessed with beauty and had a virtual model of a nine-hole golf course on her face, had been described as a "two-bagger." This meant that the man wore a bag also, in case hers blew off. The entire thing is redundant, however, for, the truth be told—and it rarely is when men gather to discuss sex—getting to a stage of having sex with any of these teenage Catholic girls was nigh on impossible. If he was lucky, a boy might get a kiss or, as they say in Dublin, a "ware." If he was very, very lucky, he might get an outside feel of a breast. But getting anywhere near the nether regions took more than luck; usually it took a gold ring.

The girls sipped on their drinks. Around the room there was female chatter everywhere. From the far side of the partition could be heard the raucous laughter of the men, the clinking of their glasses, the ringing of the tills, and in the background some man coughing and spluttering as he choked on Marion's mother's toenail. Giddy Eye had gone very quiet. Agnes figured she was sulking about Marion's patch remark. "Are you all right, Giddy Eye?" she asked.

"I'd look fucking stupid with a patch on my eye," Giddy Eye said. Agnes looked to Marion and scowled. Marion knew that look of Agnes': it was saying, Apologize now. Marion threw her eyes to heaven.

"Giddy, I was just joking about the patch," was as close as Marion was going to come to an apology. It was enough to satisfy Giddy.

"Really?" she asked the wall.

"Really," said Marion. "Sure you'd hardly notice it," she lied. "Here," said Marion, "did you hear this one?" The girls leaned in, for they knew there was a joke coming. Marion giggled, as she always did before she told a joke. She began.

"Three cross-eyed men were up in court in front of a cross-eyed judge?" The girls nodded and were smiling in anticipation. "So the judge says to the first fella, 'What's your name?' And the second fella says, 'O'Brien.' 'I wasn't talking to you,' says the judge, and the third fella said, 'I never opened me mouth.'" The girls howled with laughter. Well, two of them did. Giddy did not even crack a smile. Marion slapped her leg and said, "Ah, Giddy, it's just a joke, don't be sulking."

"I'm not," answered Giddy. "I don't get it." Now the girls screeched with laughter, a puzzled Giddy sitting there asking, "What? What?"

At about eleven-thirty Madigan's Pub began to empty. Outside, the crowds were gathered in groups, all trying to decide where they would go from here. Of course it was Marion that led the way as the four girls cut a swathe through the chattering crowd. No standing around for these four: they knew exactly where they were going. The Friday-night ritual. First they went to Fortes Fish and Chip

Shop, to satisfy Marion's addiction to fried food after every drinking session. Agnes, Giddy, and Nine Warts stood outside while Marion bought her usual fish and chips, with extra vinegar. Marion would douse the chipped potatoes with so much vinegar that as she was eating the fries out of the bag the excess vinegar would drip from between her fingers. The girls would make her walk twenty paces behind them as they made the long uphill walk along Parnell Square to the National Ballroom. Marion would continue to take part in conversations as she was walking behind the other three eating from her steaming bag, giving the impression sometimes of being a lunatic talking to herself, and crying—the vinegar and steam making her eyes water.

As they walked along that night, Giddy Eye spoke worriedly.

"I'm not going to get in here, I'm telling you I'm barred," she moaned.

"Shut up, Giddy Eye. They won't remember you. Just keep your eyes straight in front," Marion roared from behind. The other two girls giggled.

"Oops, sorry, Giddy. You know what I mean, Giddy Eye, just don't look at them and walk straight in, they won't even notice," Marion tried to explain, the vinegar tears streaming from her own eyes.

When at last they arrived at the National Ballroom, they could see a fracas happening at the stepped entrance to the ballroom. A small crowd watched. When they got closer they could see there was a young man arguing with a bouncer. The young man was making an effort to convince the bouncer that he was not drunk.

"You're drunk. Now, go away," the bouncer was saying as he tried to ease the young man back down the steps.

"I'm not drunk, I'm . . . Eh . . ." The man searched his mind for a medical condition that would meet two criteria. One, it must make him appear intoxicated. And, two, it must be easy to pronounce when you are as intoxicated as he was.

". . . I'm a bleedin' diabetic," he settled on. It might have worked had the "-ic" part of the last word not sent a splash of alcohol-tainted saliva shooting from the man's mouth right onto the chin of the bouncer. The bouncer lost it. Using just one arm, the bouncer lifted the "diabetic" down the remaining steps and sent him on his merry way. Our four girls had no such problems. Agnes had been correct. Not one bouncer gave Giddy Eye a second glance.

Once inside, the girls queued up for the cloakroom to deposit their coats. This was not only necessary for safety's sake, but also as an escape mechanism. The ballroom had lately been fitted with ultra-violet lights, which tended to make all the men standing under them appear as though they were tanned Italians. Sometimes it was not possible until one saw the man in the cold light of a normal electric bulb to realize that the "fine thing" a girl thought she had picked was actually a pale Buster Keaton look-alike. It was on the line at the end of the night to collect your coat that was the best place to discover this, and if necessary a girl could then lose herself in the crowd.

Within minutes the girls were settled at the "girls' wall," each with her glass of cola in hand. Marion scanned their immediate surroundings to be sure there were no bouncers about. When she was sure it was safe, she pulled the snifter of vodka from her bag. Wearing her elfish little grin that Agnes loved so much, Marion poured a dash of vodka into each of the girls' colas. The four happy girls tapped glasses and cried, "Cheers." As Agnes took a swig from her glass, her smile vanished and her eyes widened.

"Oh, shite, *he's* here," she spluttered.

"What?" Giddy Eye called over the music. Agnes leaned forward, and the three other girls huddled in.

"Don't look now, but it's the weirdo." Agnes glanced up, then re-entered the huddle. "He's standing over beside the third pillar." They all looked. He saw them looking and gave a smile and waved over at them. Giddy Eye and Philomena waved back.

"Will youse fuck off wavin', you'll only encourage him." Agnes turned away so her back was now to the young man.

"He's a big fella, isn't he?" Giddy Eye observed.

"Stop looking," Agnes demanded, speaking through her clenched teeth as she did so.

But they didn't stop looking. "He cleans up well, he's not bad once he gets the coal dust off'a him," Philomena announced. Agnes threw her eyes to the heavens and pretended to be looking at something very interesting on the wall.

"Uh-oh," the girls said in unison.

"What?" Agnes asked, over her shoulder.

"He's coming over," said Philomena. In one swift move Agnes put her glass on the table and grabbed Marion by the arm.

"What are you doing?" Marion cried.

"Come on, you, we're dancing," Agnes ordered.

"Will you wait a minute, for Jaysus' sake?" Marion was trying to place her glass on the table as she was being dragged toward the dance floor. Before Marion knew it, she was jiving in the middle of the heaving mass on the beechwood floor. From the corner of her eye Agnes caught sight of Tommo Monks as he stopped walking. He stood for a moment, thwarted. The smile left his face and, with his shoulders sagging in disappointment, he returned to his pillar.

Throughout the next two hours, Tommo Monks made it halfway across the floor four times. On each occasion Agnes again and again dragged Marion onto the dance floor. Then, suddenly, he was gone. His pillar was deserted. Marion was glad of the rest.

"For fuck's sake, Agnes, you have me exhausted," Marion got out through her panting breath.

"Yeh, I'm sorry. Well, at least it worked. Maybe now he got the message," Agnes said as she opened her purse and pulled out a cigarette.

"Excuse me," came a deep voice from behind Agnes. She froze, the cigarette in her lips, the lighted match just inches from the tip of it. Agnes didn't have to look behind her, she knew it was him. Tommo spoke again. "I'm sorry to interrupt you girls, and I know you must be tired, I've been watching the two of you dancing all night. But would you possibly have just one more dance in you?" His voice was slow and even. Over her shoulder, Agnes could get a faint smell of alcohol from his breath. She spun around. Her voice when it came was sharp—a mixture of being startled, and being quite pissed off that she had not fully gotten rid of the man.

"Now, listen to me, you," she spat, and stepped right up to Tommo's face. "I have been dancing all night and I'm tired all right. Now I'm going to have a smoke and a break. So, lover boy, if you don't mind I'll sit this one out." The man was blushing now, and taken aback by Agnes' outburst. He was flustered. He dropped his head and pushed his hands into his pockets.

"I'm sorry, love" he said to Agnes. "I wasn't asking you. I was asking *you*." He looked past Agnes to Marion. All three girls turned toward Marion, aghast. Marion's face lit up with a huge smile.

"Sure, Tommo, I'll dance with you."

She took his arm, and they took to the floor for a slow dance. The music played softly, and Marion pressed her face against Tommo's body, just about at his navel, the leather belt on his pants rubbing under her chin. Slowly the ever-so-mismatched pair moved in a circle around the floor. Streaks of sparkling light reflected from the gigantic crystal ball spinning in the center of the ceiling streamed across them like slow-motion fireworks. Marion beamed a huge smile over at Agnes, who was standing staring at the two, her still-unlit cigarette hanging from her lips, a black burnt-out matchstick in her hand. Tommo Monks was the happiest man in the ballroom.

He leaned down and whispered into Marion's ear, "You smell beautiful."

"Thank you," Marion cooed up to him.

"What scent is that?" he asked softly.

"Vinegar," she answered.

He smiled, and Marion closed her eyes to enjoy the moment.

CHAPTER TWENTY-EIGHT

It was a whirlwind romance. Tommo just swept Marion off her feet—not a great journey, mind you. Over the next six months, Agnes saw little of Marion except in work. She now made her visits to Dolly each Sunday alone, as Marion and Tommo were always going somewhere. A picnic on Bray Head, or a visit to the zoo, or some such. In the evenings, Agnes had just Connie to talk to and nobody to listen to. She missed Marion. At work, Nellie was getting more and more sick, so Agnes now did the wholesalers alone, and Nellie came to the stall for just a couple of hours each day. Agnes envied Marion. To have someone in your life that cared for you. Someone to share everything with. Someone who would listen and laugh at your jokes. Children. A life. She was becoming more wistful by the day.

She was standing by the stall thinking some of these thoughts when Marion interrupted her. "Penny for your thoughts," Marion said.

"They're not worth it." Agnes smiled at her friend. Marion produced a packet of cigarettes, and they both lit up and sat on the apple box.

"Nellie out again?" Marion asked, although she knew the answer.

"Yep. I don't know what's the matter with her. She won't go to a doctor and she's getting worse by the day." Agnes really was worried, this wasn't idle chat.

"So. How are you?" Marion asked.

"I'm all right."

"D'ye miss me?" Marion giggled.

But Agnes' reply was serious. "Yeh, Marion, I do. I miss you awful."

"Well, I miss you too, something terrible." Marion linked her arm into Agnes'. "I told Tommo. I said I'll see him every Monday, Friday, and Saturday. The rest of the week I'm seeing me friend Agnes." She smiled.

"Did you, Marion, really?" Agnes asked.

"Of course I did. And on Sundays, I said, we have to visit Dolly." They hugged.

"Oh, Marion, what was I like without you?" Agnes was thrilled.

"It's only right, Agnes. I can't be ignoring me chief bridesmaid," Marion said.

It took a moment for Agnes to get it. "Bridesmaid? You're not . . . !"

"I fuckin' am, Agnes Reddin. White dress, reception, the whole fuckin' nine yards!" They squealed as they hugged and danced around in a circle, burning cigarette holes in each other's cardigans.

On her next visit, Agnes told Dolly of Marion's good news. Dolly said she was pleased, but she didn't look it.

"What's wrong, Dolly?" Agnes asked.

"*What's wrong?* This is wrong, all of this. I done nothing, for fuck's sake!" She began to cry.

"Keep it down, there," a guard called.

"Oh, fuck off, you!" Dolly called back.

"What?" the guard asked as he stood.

Agnes stood also. "Nothing, sorry, we'll keep it down." The guard sat. Agnes went back to Dolly. "For Christ's sake, Dolly, calm down. Don't get him mad," she chided.

"Fuck him, and the likes of him. You only see them at the gate. Bastards! Pretending to search us and squeezing our breasts. Watching us in the showers and playing with themselves in front of us. Pushing their truncheon down your knickers and shoving it between your legs. *Bastards!*"

"*Stop!*" Agnes yelled. "Please stop, Dolly." Agnes began to weep. So did Dolly. Dolly placed her hand across the table onto Agnes' trembling hands.

"I'm sorry, Agnes, I'm just having a bad day!"

"No. I'm sorry, Dolly. You should be out of here by now. I haven't done enough to get you out." Agnes was overcome now.

"Stop, Agnes, you couldn't have done any more. Now, stop it!" They sat in silence for a while, the nightmare that was Dolly's life too big for Agnes to contemplate.

"You'd better go, Aggie. Tell Marion I wish her luck, and I do, really." Dolly got up and left the room. Agnes made her way from the room slowly. She felt completely powerless. She was.

Marion's wedding was a great affair. In her wedding dress and standing just four feet eight inches, with heels, and about the same width, Marion looked like a delivery of flour bags. But she glowed with happiness, as did her new husband. Tommo and Marion were joined together in the Church of St. Jarlath by the "new" priest, Father Pius. This attractive young priest had just returned from the missions in Africa. He stood smiling at the altar, for this was his first wedding ceremony in his native land since his ordination. The female members of the congregation watched the priest more than the happy couple. One could hardly blame them. He spoke each word of the Mass in his deep but soft tone. When he went to the tabernacle to fetch the Host, he seemed to float along in his colored vestments; with a deep tan, and his long hair slicked back with Brylcreme, he made a hundred hearts flutter. Father Pius was the only priest in the parish under sixty years of age, so he stuck out like a sore thumb. The queues for his confessional on Thursday nights were huge, while the other priests sat in theirs alone.

The wedding breakfast was held in the Clarence Hotel, and Tommo really pushed the boat out. Grapefruit cocktail, stuffed chicken breast, and sherry trifle, all devoured by the eighty or so attendants. Marion's plate had a special addition, steaming chips covered in vinegar. Agnes looked divine. She wore a lavender satin dress with a wide purple waistband and matching crown. After the meal the tables were cleared and pushed back to make room for the dancing and drinking. When the band struck up, Tommo and Marion took to the dance floor for their first dance as Mr. and Mrs. Monks. Everybody clapped, and then there was a rush of women over to the "new" priest to ask him to dance. He declined respectfully and crossed the room to ask the chief bridesmaid to dance. Agnes accepted. The dancing pair were glared at by every woman in the place, the older ones disapproving of the young priest's forward behavior and the younger ones filled with envy. When the dance finished, Agnes thanked the priest. He walked her back to her seat.

"How is your mother?" he asked. Agnes was little surprised at the question.

"The same, Father. Thanks for asking," she replied, not really giving any information.

"I have seen her down at the shops. A fine woman. Would you mind if I paid her a visit?" he asked.

"No, I wouldn't mind." Agnes was not fond of the clergy, but liked this one.

"I will, then," he said, with a smile in his voice. And he was gone, knowing that the feet would be danced off him by the night's end.

Agnes returned to her seat and to her thoughts, which were now very confused. It had nothing to do with the priest. It was the letter she had received that morning. It was typed, so she was able to read it; she had difficulty reading if the words were handwritten. She opened her handbag and took it out again. It had the large red maple leaf on the top, and in gold the words "Embassy of Canada." She read it again.

Dear Miss Agnes Reddin,

I refer to your application for an emigration visa and assisted passage to Canada, more specifically Toronto, Ontario, some time ago.

At the time of your application, this embassy informed you by post that you were below the age for consideration. However, it has been kept on file, and as you are now of the age, your application has resurfaced. Should you still have an interest, I have been asked to inform you of the following:

Pending the outcome of a medical examination, which will be paid for by this embassy, your application has been successful. You should make arrangements to have the medical check through this office within sixty days of receipt of this letter. You should also supply this embassy with your Irish passport so the visa can be attached.

Yours sincerely,
Mr. Stanley DeBruin
Visa Section

She remembered her excitement back when she had made the application, at the thought of a new life in a new place. So much had changed since that day. How could she leave now? Connie would be alone, Dolly would probably be in prison for the rest of her life. She folded the letter and placed it back in her handbag. When she looked up, he was standing right in front of her. Marion was holding him by the arm. She had ushered him over to the table.

"Agnes, I want you to meet Redser Browne," Marion announced.

"Hello," Agnes offered.

"Yo, babe!" he replied. He was a good-looker, and well dressed too.

"He's a friend of Tommo's, and he's the best jiver in the Ierne Ballroom. He was looking for someone to dance with, and I told him that you were the best one here, didn't I?" She asked the young man with the flaming red hair to confirm this.

"Yeh, she did. Do yeh wanna dance, babe, or what?"

Agnes took to the floor with Redser. Within minutes they had taken over the floor. This man could dance, and Agnes loved it! They danced and danced, taking just short breaks, during which Agnes would throw back a vodka, then back on the floor. By night's end her head was spinning, and Agnes had had the time of her life. He asked to walk her home, and Agnes was pleased.

On the way they talked a little; actually he talked, and a lot. His name was Nicholas Browne. The name Redser came for the obvious reason, his ginger mane. He was twenty-one, a year and a half older than Agnes. He used to work down in the coal yard; that's where he met Tommo. He was surprised to be invited to the bash, for he didn't really know Tommo that well, and always thought him to be a retard. Agnes didn't like this comment, but then reconciled it by admiring his honesty. By the time they reached her home, Agnes knew everything there was to know about Redser Browne. They stood outside her building.

"Well, here we are, this is me!" Agnes waved her arm across the front of the building as if it were Buckingham Palace.

"Great!" said Redser as he bounded up the steps. Before she knew it, they were sitting at the kitchen table sipping tea. Agnes was very drunk and wanted to go to bed, but Redser just carried on talking and talking. Until at last he realized he was overdoing it.

"Jaysus, I'm sorry, love. I always do that when I'm nervous. You know. Talk." He was embarrassed.

"Not at all, it's very interesting," Agnes lied. That's when it happened. Out of the blue, he leaned over and kissed her. A long kiss. She melted. He ran his hands over her body. Agnes lost track of where they were, and for a moment thought, *How many hands does this fecker have?* He laid her on the floor. And undid his zipper, producing his member.

"What the fuck is that?" Agnes asked in a small terrified voice.

"Yeh babe, it's big, isn't it!" he boasted.

"No, really, what is it?" Agnes asked. She had never seen a grown man's penis before. Too late. In the next ten minutes, Agnes lost her virginity on the floor of her mother's home. It all happened so fast that she didn't fully understand what had happened. She was so confused, she felt dreadful about doing "it," but at the same time she loved it. Somebody wanted her and it felt good . . . or bad. Five minutes later, Redser was gone. Agnes bathed herself until the water went cold. She spent her time in bed equally between smiling and sobbing through the night.

CHAPTER TWENTY-NINE

Father Pius kept his word and became a regular visitor to Connie. She never once recognized him as a priest or even a friend. He found he had to reintroduce himself every other visit. He didn't mind. He enjoyed the visits; if nothing else, they kept him busy. He needed to keep busy; he was finding it difficult to settle in his new parish. After the relaxed environment he had enjoyed in Africa, the parish house felt like a prison.

The Church of St. Jarlath is a very settled and conservative church. Surrounded by its huge population that is packed with Catholics, it has a ready audience. Each Sunday, all of the Masses were packed, so in their complacency the older priests of the church were very set in their ways. Father Murphy *always* said ten o'clock Mass, Father Augustus *always* eleven o'clock Mass, and Father Angelus *always* twelve o'clock Mass. There was no nine o'clock Mass, as that was when the priests were usually having their breakfast. So, for the early morning Mass-goers, there was only the seven-thirty Mass. All three of the older priests hated doing the seven-thirty Mass. Usually the priests took turns in saying the early one, along with their own Mass later. This way they would only have to do it once every three Sundays. Now, with the arrival of a new young priest, they could all sleep a little later each Sunday and leave the early Mass to the "young buck." Lowest in the pecking order and all that. The new priest, Father Pius, didn't mind this at all, his only gripe being that once his seven-thirty Mass was fin-ished he had the whole day ahead of him and little to do. So, at breakfast one morning, he asked the elderly priests if there was any way he could assist them in their Masses. They all looked at him and then at each other, the same thought going through all of their heads *Share the altar? No chance.* Father Pius knew that this was what they would be thinking and immediately allayed their fears. "I'm not talking about sharing the altar or anything like that. But I must be able to help in some way? I play the organ, you know."

The priests all exhaled with relief. "Oh, the organ; well, then, why don't you play at my Mass?" Father Murphy asked graciously.

"*Really*, Father, could I?"

"Absolutely," Father Murphy replied, and they all went back to their breakfast. Well, if Father Pius thought the priests were set in their ways, it was nothing to what was to come. For the lay people who served the church were even more set. Father Pius was to dis-cover this when he arrived at the organ the following Sunday to perform at Father Murphy's Mass. Here he met for the first time Johnny Brennan. Johnny had been pumping the organ at St. Jar-lath's for forty years. Father Pius introduced himself and Johnny grunted, didn't shake hands, and just waved him away.

"I know, I know who you are. I saw you saying your Mass last week." He winked at the priest. "Nice and quick, good man, keep it moving."

"Any requests?" Father Pius asked. Johnny looked at him with a puzzled face.

"Requests? What are you feckin' talking about?"

"I just thought you might like me to play something. I mean, is there anything that you particularly like to hear in the church?"

"Aye." He nodded toward the congregation. "The sound of them feckers' feet all leaving. That's what I like to hear, Father. Now, sit down there like a good man and don't be boring the arse off me." Johnny disappeared behind the organ to prepare the pump.

Smiling to himself, Father Pius sat down at the huge keyboard. He turned and pulled at the knobs, setting the strings, bass, and rhythm to his own liking. Father Pius loved playing religious music. But he also loved experimenting, sticking in a little "twiddle" at the end of this eight-bar or a little "toodle" at the top of the next. It made it different and a little bit more enjoyable for him and, he hoped, the recipients of the music. With his right hand he did a quick up and down the scales, adding a little jazz riff at the bottom of the scale. He looked over his shoulder. The congregation were seated. There were three minutes to Mass. He thought he would begin with "Adeste Fideles." A beautiful hymn. He turned back to the keyboard to see the head of Johnny Brennan peeping out from behind the keys. Father Pius jumped, startled.

"Was that you?" Johnny asked.

"Sorry?" Father Pius said.

"That racket, was that you? Did you fall on the keyboard?"

"No, I was just . . . I'm sorry," Father Pius apologized.

"Right, let's get it going, then. What's it to be?" Johnny asked.

"'Adeste Fideles,'" Father Pius said.

"Oh, right," said Johnny and off he went. Father Pius began to play, and Johnny began to pump. Father Pius wasn't quite sure, but if memory served him right, "Adeste Fideles" was about three minutes and twenty seconds long. There were now two and a half minutes to go to the beginning of Mass, and it would be nice to finish just as the serving priest was genuflecting at the altar. So off he went, glancing up at the small mirror in which he could see the altar. He played beautifully, and indeed the twiddles and toodles added to the piece. Then, suddenly, with about a quarter of the piece left, the organ died. Father Pius leaned over and pulled some of the switches, trying to check the vents, valves, and reeds. Everything seemed to be all right. He heard the congregation stand as the priest arrived at the altar. Too late to start again now. He left his seat and went around to the back of the organ. Johnny Brennan was sitting on the pump, smoking a cigarette.

"The organ, it stopped. What happened?" he asked Johnny.

"It's finished, the piece is finished," Johnny answered, taking a drag from his smoke.

"No, it wasn't finished, there was a good quarter of the piece to go." Father Pius spoke in a hushed voice.

Johnny Brennan stood and walked to the priest and stood face to face with him. "Father, there is five hundred and sixty-one pumps in 'Adeste Fideles,' and you have fuckin' had them." He walked back to the pump and sat to finish his smoke.

Hard as it was, Father Pius was settling in nonetheless. The invitation to celebrate the wedding of Tommo and Marion and then to join the party later was just what he needed to touch base with the younger members of the parish.

His visiting of Connie was a different matter. Even though he could see that Connie did not know who he was, he enjoyed making her tea and listening to the stories that came in fragments from her lips.

CHAPTER THIRTY

Redser Browne, it turned out, was a tonic. He had a wonderful sense of humor and made Agnes laugh a lot. Mind you, she didn't see too much of Redser over the next few weeks, she was too busy. She saw him on the Thursday night after the wedding. He took her to the dog track on race night, where Agnes had an amazing streak of luck.

They had settled themselves in a seat near the bar. Redser gave Agnes a race card, which she thought was silly because the dogs were numbered one through six in every race. From where they sat they could see the dogs for the first race walk around the parade ring.

"There they are!" Redser pointed out. He then went on to describe the betting system. There was a forecast, where you pick the first two dogs to cross the line, or you could reverse that, in which case it didn't matter which way they finished as long as they were the correct two dogs. He went on to describe the trio, triella, with the field, without the favorite, lucky four, super six, all in great detail. At the end of this, Agnes still had no idea what he was talking about and she handed him two shillings.

"Number four to win," is all she said.

He was a little disappointed that she was not going for one of the creative bets he had described. "Okay. Why did you pick number four?" he asked, scanning the form of the number-four dog in the program.

"I watched him in the parade ring. Just before he left it he had a piss. I always find that if I do that before I leave the house I walk much faster, don't you?" Redser stared at her for a moment.

"Yeh. Sure. Number four to win." Redser returned just minutes before the "off." He handed Agnes her ticket. He was holding a huge bunch of tickets for himself.

"Jaysus, how many bets have you done?" Agnes asked when she saw the bunch. Redser just winked and smiled.

"You have to cover your arse with these bookies." He held up the bunch. "Whoever wins, I'm covered." Redser was covered in most ways, except if number four won—which he did, by a long way, to Agnes' shrieks of delight.

"I won, I won, did you see that? I won. Wasn't he brilliant?" she cried with delight.

"Yeh. Fantastic," replied Redser unenthusiastically, tossing his bundle of tickets on the ground. Redser went and got himself another bundle of tickets and of course did Agnes' bet, which was? Yes. Number four to win. Which it did, again. And again, and again. Remarkably, the dogs wearing number four won the first five races in a row. Agnes was delirious. By race number five, Redser was depressed. He selected his combinations of dogs yet again, and prepared to leave to place his bets, not before putting his hand out for Agnes' two shillings.

"Let me guess?" he said to her. "Number four to win again?"

"No way," Agnes replied. "He'll be exhausted by now." She smiled a knowing smile. Redser was fit only for suicide at this point.

Marion returned from her honeymoon at Butlin's Holiday Camp and settled into the flat that Tommo had rented in a tenement just around the corner from Agnes. On one of their tea breaks sitting on the apple boxes, the ugly subject of sex came up.

"Tommo was very nervous, Agnes!" Marion began. "He wouldn't take his clothes off at first. So I helped him." They giggled.

"Marion, were you not even a little scared?" Agnes asked, recalling her own discomfort with Redser.

"No. Not at first. Not until I pulled down his underpants. My Jaysus! Agnes, I nearly fuckin' died." She looked about her, checking for eavesdroppers. She went on. "His mickey! Agnes, it was bigger than me!"

Agnes howled with laughter, the look of shock on Marion's face making the story all the more funny. "I know." Agnes laughed. "It's huge!"

Marion stopped and stared at Agnes. "What do you mean?" Marion asked.

Agnes stopped laughing abruptly. "What?" She blushed.

"You said, 'I know.' How do you know?" Marion was suspicious.

Agnes was flustered. "I didn't mean I knew about Tommo's mickey, I meant in general. Men's mickeys are huge! That's all," she explained. Marion continued to stare. Agnes was getting more uncomfortable. "What? Why are you looking at me like that?" Agnes was decidedly mortified now.

"You done it! Didn't you?" Marion accused. The truth is that Marion never for one moment suspected that Agnes had been with Tommo. She was just shocked that Agnes would even consider sex before marriage.

"No. Shut up!"

"You did. Who was it?" Marion had a little smile now. She was enjoying Agnes' discomfort. Agnes did not reply. They sat in silence for a few moments, Agnes wanting the conversation to go away and Marion deep in thought.

"REDSER," Marion accused. "Redser Browne." Marion could tell from the look on Agnes' face that she had hit the nail on the head. She began to laugh and laugh. Agnes dived on her, trying to put her hand over Marion's mouth. Marion pretended to make an announcement. "Agnes lost her cherry!" she tried to get out through Agnes' hand. They wrestled with each other among the empty cardboard boxes, both laughing so much it hurt.

"You two, stop that!" It was Marion's mother calling to them. They wrestled on. "Stop it now, both of you!" It was a scream now from Mrs. Delany, and she was pulling roughly at Agnes to get her off Marion. They stopped wrestling and stood brushing themselves off. Mrs. Delany's scream had startled them.

"Jaysus, Mammy, what's wrong with yeh? We were just having a bit of fun!" Marion said to her mother.

Mrs. Delany looked pained. "Well, it's no time for fun. Agnes, you must go down to the Mater Hospital—now! It's urgent. Marion, you go with her and take care of her."

CHAPTER THIRTY-ONE

It was the first Sunday Agnes had not visited Dolly. But Dolly understood. She was only too aware how much Nellie Nugent had meant to Agnes. Dolly had asked to get released for the funeral on the Sunday but was refused. Only events concerning direct and immediate family would be considered for a temporary release. So instead she stayed after Mass in the prison chapel and prayed for her.

At the funeral Mass in St. Jarlath's, Father Pius told the assembled traders that he knew very little about Nellie, which put him in the same boat as the rest of them. "But I do know this," he went on, "our biggest fear in this life is that we will end up alone. That we will pass from this life and nobody will notice, or care." He now looked directly at Agnes. "Nellie Nugent was not alone. And someone does care. Now, as she sits with our heavenly Father, safe in His care, she knows for sure that here in our mortal world, a world full of pain and grief, she was loved, very much loved!"

Agnes thanked Father Pius after the Mass for his beautiful words. She was very sad. He took her hand and squeezed it.

"Agnes, you still have your mother," he tried to console her.

She gave a tiny smile in recognition of his effort. "No, I haven't, Father. Not for a long, long time. But thanks!"

They laid Nellie to rest in Glasnevin Cemetery, the burial attended by more friends than she knew she had.

* * * * *

Nellie's death was the catalyst. So much needed to be done. First, Agnes went to the Canadian Embassy for her interview. It went well, and they made an appointment for her to take her medical three weeks later. The next step was to get a passport. Agnes got the relevant forms from the police station and filled them in as best she could. She literally tore the flat apart looking for the photographs. They were school ones, but Agnes was sure that she looked old enough in them to pass. She found them in, of all places, her mother's bedside drawer. She took the photographs and the form to the police station, where the form was stamped. The policeman passed comment on the photographs: "You are a lot younger here," he said.

"I know, they're school ones. I didn't want to spend the money on new ones if I didn't have to," Agnes explained.

"Oh, you can tell it's you all right; I was just saying, that's all. Where are you going, then?"

"Canada. I'm emigrating there," she said with a broad smile.

"Good for you. I have a cousin in Nova Scotia. He's there ten years. Loves it! You're dead right, love. Make a good life for yourself." He stamped the photos, and the form.

"Just bring all of that to the passport office and they'll do it all for you. And good luck to you!" He smiled.

"Thanks," Agnes answered.

Agnes told nobody except Marion about the Canada thing. Not even Redser, whom she continued to see and was getting quite fond of. Sure, he was as rough as a bear's arse, but in other ways he was a good man. They went to the pictures, or for a drink, and only occasionally to the dog track—Redser still went to the track every week but only took Agnes the odd time. She now waited for her passport to come and for her medical. In the meantime, she worked the stall just as hard as before, taking as much as she could in cash, and saving as never before. When the passport arrived, she was delighted.

Marion screamed with laughter at the photograph.

"Of course, you never had a school photograph, did you?" Agnes jeered.

"It would have to have been a very fast camera," said Marion, laughing.

Agnes left the passport at the embassy next day. They explained that once Agnes had cleared the medical they would attach the visa and she would have ninety days to enter Canada to make it official.

Ninety days. That was the problem. She knew from the start that the plan could only go so far. But Agnes had hoped that by the time she had everything organized she would have come up with an idea to finish the plan off. She hadn't. It was just five days to her medical, and then she would have just ninety days. Could she pull it off in ninety days? It didn't seem likely; frankly, it seemed impossible. She went into a depression. Marion tried to cheer her up, but to no avail. She was stressed out and began to throw up every time she thought of the ninetieth day arriving. She was snapping at everyone, and this month her period pains were worse than ever, she was doubled in pain. Visiting Dolly was now so painful—sitting there exchanging benign conversation, and desperately trying not to mention Canada, or even hint that there was anything going on. In all the planning and hard work, it never once crossed Agnes' mind that she might not pass the medical. She had never been sick, she had never attended a doctor, and she felt fine. In any case, the medical day came, and no amount of planning could prepare her for what was to transpire. The medical would solve her Canada dilemma once and for all.

• • • • •

She was not expecting the doctor to be so handsome, the first one anyway. Agnes was to be seen by three doctors. A general practitioner, a specialist, and an ENT doctor. The handsome one was the GP, Dr. O'Reilly. She first gave a urine sample. Then a nurse took a blood sample from her. Then it got embarrassing. She had to strip naked and wear a flimsy gown. Over the next half-hour, she was weighed, probed, squeezed, and measured. She was glad when it was all over. It had exhausted her.

For some reason Agnes had thought that she would leave the doctors and the result of her medical would be posted to her. So she was quite surprised when the nurse asked her to wait in the reception area for a few minutes and Dr. O'Reilly would have preliminary results for her. She flipped through a magazine as she waited. It was an American movie magazine. Full of pictures of the stars, Marlon Brando, Grace Kelly, Anna Magnani, whom she had loved in *The Rose Tattoo*. Time passed, and she was called into Dr. O'Reilly's office. He sat behind his desk wearing a huge smile.

"Sit down, Agnes!" he invited. She thought *Oh, we're on first names now, are we? I suppose it's only to be expected from a man that has just had his rubber-clad finger up your rectum.* She sat. He closed the file he had been reading.

"Well, I'm sure you are anxious to hear the result. Sometimes this is the part of the whole process I hate. For I must sit across from a person filled with hope and disappoint them. I don't like doing that." He leaned back in his chair.

Agnes wasn't sure what game he was playing, but she wasn't having any part of it. "Did I fuckin' pass or what?" she asked directly. Taking the wind out of his sails.

He leaned forward. "Yes. You passed, and with flying colors, I might add." He smiled.

Agnes smiled too. She relaxed. "Thank you, doctor, can I go now?" she asked, anxious to get back to her stall.

"Of course, we are all finished here. I'll send the results on to the visa section. I'm sorry the examination was so uncomfortable. It's a demand of the Canadian Embassy, no stone left unturned and all that," he apologized. He stood and opened the door.

Agnes reddened. "Yeh, no stone," is all she could think to say, as she made for the door.

"Of course, it would have been helpful if you had told us at the start that you were pregnant," he said as a side comment.

Agnes froze on the spot. She went pale and, still staring at the doctor, keeled over in a faint.

When she came to, Agnes was lying on the doctor's couch. A nurse was calling her name. Agnes could see a glass of water in the nurse's hand. She took it and gulped on it. The doctor was sitting at the end of the couch, he had a worried look on his face.

"Agnes?" he called. "Are you awake, Agnes?" he tried again. To Agnes he sounded like he was at the far end of a tunnel. Her head cleared some more, and she gulped on the water again.

"I'm okay!" she told them.

"Agnes, the pregnancy makes no difference. It will not affect your application in any way." the doctor was trying to reassure her.

"No difference?" Agnes asked. "Then *you* have the fuckin' baby! Of course it makes a difference!" she screamed.

CHAPTER THIRTY-TWO

Agnes waited for Redser to say something, anything. He stood ten feet in front, facing away from her, so she couldn't even see his expression. It was so quiet that she could hear the tiny *plip* sound the remains of the rainwater, from the shower earlier, was making as it dripped from the roof of the railway arch they stood under to the puddles on the ground. They were walking back from the dog track, where Redser had lost all his money and a good portion of Agnes' too. She had no idea of how to break it gently, so she just said it: "I'm pregnant!" Now she waited for his reaction. When he spoke he did so without turning.

"We'd better get married so!" he said quietly.

"Really?" Agnes enthused.

"Yeh. Why not? I have a friend that gets rings, I'll get you one tomorrow." And it was set; well, nearly.

"I don't want a ring. I want a bicycle. I'll get some use out of that," Agnes said, and in her own practical world, this made sense.

The next day, she told Marion about both the pregnancy and the wedding. Marion was more pleased about the pregnancy than the wedding.

"Are you sure, Agnes? You only know him a while." Marion, truth be told, did not like Redser Browne.

"Of course I'm sure. He's the father of me child. Of course I'm sure," Agnes said. She didn't sound it.

"What about the Canada plan?" Marion asked.

"I have it all worked out," Agnes said. They lit up a cigarette, and Agnes went over her thoughts with Marion.

Redser was such a stupid oaf! Agnes had drummed it into him all the way as they had walked up to the church residence to see Father Pius. "Don't mention the pregnancy, don't mention the pregnancy!" How much clearer can you get?

Just ten minutes into the interview and Father Pius made the standard comment: "Are you both sure you do not want to wait a little longer to think about this? Marriage is a big step!"

As Agnes was smiling and shaking her head, Redser said, "We can't, sure she's due in November!"

A stunned silence followed. Father Pius looked at his fingers, waiting for an explanation. "Ow!" Redser exclaimed. "You're hurting me." He pulled his arm away from Agnes' grip.

"So, then, Agnes, you are pregnant?" Father Pius asked.

"Yes," she answered quietly.

Redser looked at Agnes with surprise. "What did you tell him for?" Redser asked. Agnes glared at him. "What? What?" He didn't get it. He now turned his attention to Father Pius. "Does this mean we can't get married in the church, Father?" he asked.

"No. It doesn't mean that. You can be married in the church, just Agnes may not wear white," he said.

Agnes' eyes widened. "I am wearing white, Father," she stated.

"You can't, Agnes. That's the law. You can't." Father Pius was adamant.

"You don't understand, Father. My wedding dress has been waiting for me since the day I was born. My mother wore it, her mother
wore it, and I will be wearing it." Agnes was just as adamant.

"Listen to me, Agnes . . ." Father Pius began.

"No, you listen to me, Father. My mother walked down that
aisle in this dress to marry my father, and I will be walking down it
to marry Redser. You stand there on that altar before God and refuse to marry us? Then on your head be it." Agnes stood and took
Redser by the hand. They were leaving.

"I was going to wear a herringbone suit, Father, would that be
all right?" Redser just managed to say before Agnes dragged him
through the door.

By the end of the next day, everybody in Moore Street knew of the
upcoming marriage. And, thanks to the grapevine that was the
Jarro, everybody knew about the white dress, and everybody had an
opinion on it.

Agnes told Dolly on her next visit about everything, the pregnancy, the wedding, and the dress. It was a lot to get into a half-
hour. Dolly was fully behind Agnes.

"I wish I could be there to support you," Dolly said.

Now the good news. Agnes had waited for Dolly to say something
like that, or she would have burst. "You will be," she said simply.

"What?" Dolly's eyes began to fill up.

"I brought a copy of the banns and the license to the governor.
He has granted you two days' parole to come to the wedding," Agnes
told her. It was hard to believe that this was good news, for they both
just sat and cried for the ten minutes that remained of the visit.

◆ ◆ ◆ ◆ ◆

Over the next few weeks, Father Pius made several approaches to Agnes in an effort to get her to abandon the dress. But to no avail. He wrote to the bishop for guidance and received just orders. He spoke to the other priests in the parish about it; to a man, they refused to be drawn into it. He was alone.

Soon the day arrived.

CHAPTER THIRTY-THREE

St. Jarlath's Parish House, 3:00 a.m.

The priest's staring eyes darted away from the candle flame for just an instant. It was a reaction to the sound of the grandfather clock's first chime. The following two chimes, just like the first, were barely audible, for the clock was downstairs, in the hallway at the bottom of the great oak stairway, two floors below Father Pius' bedroom in the parish residence. The bedroom was small, but cozy. This was thanks to the furnishings Father Pius had installed there. The room was now very different from when he had arrived into it on his first day at the residence. Then the room had looked more like a cell. That had been just two years earlier. He had been so delighted to come home. Africa is a beautiful continent and his mission had been greatly rewarding, but six years was enough. Now he was home, in Dublin, beautiful Dublin.

Father Pius knew he would not sleep that night. Instead he would sit in silent, agonizing debate with his God, whom he loved so much. He sat by his bed and stared once again as the steady flame burned. In his right hand he held a Bible. As he sat there in the early hours, staring at the flame, the thumb of his left hand flicked the pages of the Bible like the poker player concentrating would do to an idle deck of cards. It made a ripping sound. In his mind he cursed his God for entrusting the mission of His Word to mere mortal men. Then he apologized. Slowly his head bowed down, and as he exhaled he muttered, "Christ!" He opened the cover of the

Bible, for no reason. This particular Bible had been given to him, a gift from the children of the mud-hut village where his mission had been based. It was a farewell gift. He came upon the inscription, written on the day of his departure by the village chief. It was in Urdu, but he read it aloud in English:

"The journey of life is a circle, from which, once embarked upon, no man can return unchanged."

He closed the cover.

"Well, that's fuck-all use," he said aloud, and he tossed it onto the bed. He closed his eyes, and in his mind he went over the possible scenario yet again.

(1) The young Agnes would walk down the aisle and stand before him.
(2) Her intended husband, Redser, would take her hand.
(3) They would probably smile.
(4) Now he, Father Pius would . . . would . . .

Would *what?* Ask her was she pregnant? No. He *knew* she was pregnant, the entire parish knew she was pregnant, the bishop knew she was pregnant. So *what*, then? What was he to do?

He stood and walked to the window, which looked out over the tenement buildings of the parish. From his pocket he took a packet of cigarettes. He lit one up and slowly blew the match out. He leaned against the window frame. From the corner of his eye he saw the letter lying open on the dressing table. He leaned over and picked it up. It bore the crest of the bishop and the address of the bishop's palace, and it was very, very clear. If the girl wore white he was instructed to refuse her the sacrament of marriage, end of story. If not he would be defrocked. He placed the letter back on the dressing table and returned to his chair. Again he picked up the

Bible and opened the page to the inscription, and again he read the inscription inside aloud.

"No, still don't fucking get it." He went back to his candle and his thoughts.

It was going to be a long night.

Agnes' home, 3:00 a.m.

Agnes sat smoking at the only table in the room. She was on her fifth cup of tea and her tenth smoke. Along with the two bedrooms, the room Agnes sat in made up the entire accommodation of the flat. Agnes had lived here since her birth twenty years ago. A lot of water had passed beneath the Ha'penny Bridge since then, and tomorrow her wedding day would be a tidal wave. She sucked on her cigarette. The glowing white wedding dress hung from the lintel over the hall door. She rubbed her tummy as she looked the dress over once again.

"I hope both of us can fit into this bloody dress," she spoke to her embryo.

She had not even tried the dress on for size. She didn't need to. It was *her* wedding dress. It had been waiting for her for twenty years.

Agnes heard some movement from the bedrooms. It drew her attention from the dress. Slowly her mother's bedroom door opened, and an ancient-looking woman shuffled out. The woman was wearing a full-length cotton nightgown, and her tiny head was covered with a red satin scarf that Agnes had tied around it earlier to keep her mother's curlers in. The woman did not speak to Agnes; she just shuffled to the kitchenette and began opening cupboards.

"What are you doing, Mammy?" Agnes asked.

"I slept late," the woman answered, a bit of panic in her voice.

"No, you didn't. It's not morning yet, Mammy, go back to bed."

"I can't, I have to prepare your father's lunchbox." The woman had already taken bread from the cupboard, the butter dish was on the counter, and she was rummaging in a drawer for a knife. Agnes stood and went to her mother. She replaced the bread and butter dish in the larder and took her mother's hand gently from the door.

"Daddy's dead, Mammy. A long time now," Agnes said, and began to guide her mother to a chair by the table. When the older woman was seated, Agnes went back to the cooker and turned the heat up under the stewing pot of tea.

"I'll pour you a cup of tea, Mammy."

"That's nice," was the reply.

"I had a maidservant, you know," Agnes' mother said to nobody in particular.

"Yes, Mammy, I know." Agnes stirred the sugar into the tea and carried it to the table. She placed the mug in front of her mother and went to sit, but her mother, in a surprisingly rapid movement, gripped Agnes' arm. She pulled her daughter toward her until their faces were just inches apart, then, with her wrinkled hand, her wedding ring barely hanging on, she stroked her daughter's cheek.

"I love you, dear," she whispered.

"I love you too, Mammy," Agnes whispered back and gently kissed her mother on the forehead. She sat.

"Drink up that tea now, Mammy, and go back to bed."

"Yes, I must. Big day tomorrow. The wedding."

Agnes was surprised that her mother remembered. "Yes, the wedding," she replied.

Agnes' mother took a sip of her tea and pointed to Agnes' bedroom door. "What's that noise?" she asked.

"I think the cow is calving." Agnes laughed; so did her mother, but the poor woman didn't know why. Agnes laughed because behind that bedroom door, asleep, lay her best friend and bridesmaid-to-be, Marion Delany. And, indeed, listening to Marion's snoring, grunting, moaning, groaning, and farting, one could think that it was indeed a cow giving birth.

Still smiling, Agnes stood.

"Come on, Mammy, let's get you back to bed." But her mother didn't move. Her eyes were downcast. Agnes stooped.

"Is the bed wet, Mammy?" she asked softly, and her mother nodded.

"That's that bloody dog again," Agnes said and stood erect. "I'm sorry, Mammy, I'll try and keep him out of your room."

"It's all right, dear, the poor animal doesn't mean it."

"I'll just go and turn the mattress and change the sheet." Agnes took a clean sheet from the linen box and went to her mother's bedroom, on the way meeting Marion coming out of *her* bedroom, wiping her eyes of sleep.

"What fucking dog? You don't have a dog," Marion said sleepily.

"Shut up, Marion," Agnes said before vanishing through her mother's bedroom door.

"Okay," Marion replied, and made for the teapot.

In the bedroom, Agnes stripped the bed and turned the mattress. It was the turning of the mattress that reminded Agnes. Quickly she left the room and went to her own bedroom. On the way she noticed Marion, now with tea in hand, sitting and chatting with her mother. When she got into her own bedroom, Agnes made her way around the window side of the room. She knew it would be there, but she felt compelled to check. She lifted the corner of the mattress and, yes, it was there. A large cream-colored envelope stuffed with papers. Agnes dropped the mattress and returned to the kitchen. Here her now excited mother introduced her to Marion.

"Agnes, this is Shirley Starlight, we've just met."

"Hello," Marion said, and flapped her eyelashes.

"Shirley has just been telling me she is a model from France," Agnes' mother went on, "a *most* interesting girl. Shirley's been married four times and all to film actors."

Scowling at Marion, Agnes took her mother's arm. "Come on, Mammy, your bed is ready." She brought her mother into her bed and tucked her in.

On her return to the kitchenette, she found Marion reclined across the table. In her cotton nightie Marion looked like a sack of spuds. She spoke with as close to a French accent as she would ever get: "'allo, I am a model; would you like to paint my titties?"

Agnes burst into laughter and dived onto Marion. She wrestled her to the floor, where they rolled around for some minutes before Agnes pinned Marion down.

"Give up?" Agnes asked.

"Okay, bitch" Marion gasped.

They laughed as Agnes rolled off Marion, and they lay there side by side, staring at the ceiling, both exhausted. It was just like they had done as children. Lying there in St. Stephen's Green and staring at the sky, the sweet smell of freshly cut grass filling their nostrils. They would lie there for hours, swapping dreams. Now there was no sky, just a ceiling, and the wedding dress.

With the telepathic shorthand that only friends know, Marion spoke first. "What are you going to do?"

"I don't know."

"He won't marry you, Agnes. He's a nice priest but he's a priest. He'll just turn you away."

"We'll see."

"Why make a fuss? Fuck it. Wear a suit and get it over with." Marion sat up. Agnes joined her. "It's my dress. It's the dress I've been waiting to wear since I was a child. My christening robe was cut from it, Dolly's christening robe was cut from it. Both of our

Communion dresses were cut from it, and by Jaysus, I am going to be married in it."

Marion placed her arm around her friend's shoulders. "Well, Mrs. *Browne*, whatever happens, you know I'll be beside you all the way." The two girls hugged.

After they brushed themselves off, Marion took the three used teacups to the sink, rinsed them under the water, and then left them upside down draining on the draining board. As she was wiping her hands in the towel, she asked, "Does your mother know about Dolly?"

"No. Jesus, she didn't even know Dolly is in prison. No, she knows nothing." Agnes put her hands to her head. "Oh Jesus, we've to do *that* today as well. Here, come on, Marion, we'd better get some sleep."

The two young women went to bed. Marion was dead to the world as soon as her head touched the pillow. Agnes sat and looked at her. A smile on her face.

It was now 3:45 a.m. by the clock on Agnes' mother's bedside table, and she was wide awake.

Connie had not said so, but she had seen the wedding dress hanging on the door lintel in the other room. It made her happy, so happy. That dress was such a part of her own journey from then to now. Such a part. Smiling from ear to ear, Agnes' mother rocked back and forth, sitting up in her bed; she was softly humming to herself. One could see in her eyes that she was not "there."

Agnes did not sleep. Instead she sat listening to Marion's cycle of grunts and farts and stared out of the window. She saw the sun rise slowly. The golden rays creeping up from the bottom of her bed. When it shines on my face I'll get up, she thought. When it shines on my face.

CHAPTER THIRTY-FOUR

Father Pius had guessed correctly; he did not sleep. He had prayed a little and smoked a lot. The ashtray, now overflowing, was testament to that. He reached for yet another one from his pack. Empty. He crushed the pack and tossed it toward the rubbish can. It missed by a lot. He made the decision to give it one more try. One last effort to get Agnes to see sense. Donning his jacket, he made his way quietly down the oak staircase and slipped out the door, closing the door gently behind him. He trotted down the granite steps and had gone no more than a hundred yards before he met a large, burly-looking man.

"Morning, Father," the man said, and tipped his cap.

"Morning," Father Pius replied. The man passed, and Father Pius spun to call after him. "Excuse me?" the priest called.

The man turned and walked back to the priest, removing his cap as he did. "Yes, Father?"

"Could I trouble you for a cigarette?" Father Pius asked.

"Certainly, Father." The man dug his hand into the heavy docker's jacket he was wearing and came up with a twenty-pack. He removed three from the pack and handed them to the priest. "Here you go, Father, you may as well have a couple, you won't get a shop open for at least an hour yet." The man then produced some matches and struck one, which he held in cupped hands for the priest to get a light. As the priest was lighting up, the man stared at him. "Do I know you?" the man asked.

"Well, are you from the parish?" Father Pius answered his question with a question.

"I am, but, begging your pardon, Father, I don't use the church, if you know what I mean. No, I mean do I know you from somewhere else?" the man asked, scrutinizing the priest's face more now.

"I doubt it," answered the priest. He took a pull on the cigarette and blew out a hearty puff.

The man replaced his cap. "Right, then, must be off. Some of us have to work for a living." And he was gone. Father Pius looked after the man. "P. J. Williams, if memory serves me," Father Pius said to himself, and then he too took off, but in the opposite direction. By the time Father Pius had reached Agnes' building, he had more or less formed his final argument in his mind. He took a deep breath and entered the building. It was quiet inside, so he made an effort to climb the stairs to Agnes' flat as quietly as possible. When he reached her door, he was about to knock when he heard a burst of laughter from behind the door. His closed fist stopped just inches from the door, and he listened. He could hear the sound of rough-and-tumble playing. And then silence—well, just panting of breaths. When they spoke he recognized the voices of Agnes and Marion.

"Jesus, I'm getting married," he heard Agnes softly say.

"Yeh," her friend answered.

"In that white dress." Agnes' voice was determined.

"But first . . . ?" It was Marion he heard now. Then they said a name together:

"*Dolly!*"

Moments later, Father Pius was back on the street on his way home. He had not the stomach for it. He needed more cigarettes.

♦ ♦ ♦ ♦ ♦

Dolly was released at 9:30 a.m. that morning for her two-day parole. She would board a bus to Dublin, which would get into Busaras, the city's main bus station, at 11:45 a.m.

The bus arrived exactly on time. Agnes and Marion were there to meet it. In her bag Agnes had the yellow package she had slept on for weeks. They watched as the passengers disembarked.

When Dolly appeared in the doorway, they both cried out her name: *"Dolly!"* They ran to each other. The three girls hugged in a huddle, laughing and crying at the same time.

"Come on, let's go to the café and have a cup of tea and a smoke," was Agnes' suggestion.

Marion wasn't sure. "Agnes, watch the time," she cautioned.

"We have time, don't worry, we have time, come on!"

The three went for tea.

"What are you talking about, no time? The wedding isn't for four and a quarter hours yet," Dolly said.

Marion looked about suspiciously. Agnes took Dolly by the shoulders and looked into her face. "Dolly, you are not going to the wedding." Dolly frowned, confused. "And you are not going back to that place either!" Agnes said this through her teeth.

Dolly shook her head. "You're crazy, Agnes. They'll come and get me. Even if I hide, they'll find me, they will; no, I'm going back." Dolly was afraid. Afraid to believe that she might have a chance at freedom.

"They won't find you where you are going. Come on, let's get some tea and I'll explain everything." They made their way to a table, and there was no further conversation until they had been served. Then Agnes produced the yellow envelope. The first thing she took from it was the passport. She slid it across the table to Dolly. Dolly opened it and was amazed. The name on it was Agnes Reddin, but the picture was Dolly. Her last one from school.

"How did you do this?" She was still in shock.

"It was easy. Here, look at this!" Agnes said as she flipped through the pages of the passport until she came to the visa for Canadian residency. "You are going to Canada!" Agnes announced.

"When?" Dolly asked. Both Marion and Agnes looked up at the clock.

"In three hours," Agnes said and smiled. She then produced a flight ticket. And a bundle of Canadian dollars.

"There's three hundred dollars there; that should get you started. Now, when you get to Canada, you will make your way to the New Residents Desk in Toronto Airport. They will bring you to your accommodation and introduce you to the person who will help you get a job. It's all written down in this letter from the embassy, you can read it on the flight." Agnes put everything back into the envelope again. She was pleased that her plan had worked out. Dolly began to cry. Marion took the cue and stood.

"I'll go for a little walk." She left the sisters alone. When she was gone, Agnes put both of her hands on Dolly's.

"It's going to be okay. A new life, a new place, new people, and a new start," she said.

Dolly held the envelope out to Agnes. "But this is *your* dream! *Always* your dream!" she said through sobs.

"I can't go, Dolly. There's Mammy, there's Redser, a new baby, the stall, a million reasons why I can't go. But you can. And you only need one reason . . . freedom! Yes, it is my dream, but I can still get something from it. You live it! Please, Dolly, you live my dream, for both of us." Agnes was barely able to speak now.

"I love you, Agnes," Dolly said.

"Then go, go to Canada, for I swear to God, Dolly Reddin, if you go back to that place I will surely die of heartbreak." Agnes was deadly serious.

"I'll go," Dolly said.

"Thank you, Dolly. And I love you too." Agnes smiled. Marion arrived back at the table.

"Come on, you two, the airport bus is leaving in three minutes. Oh and, Dolly, here," Marion said as she handed Dolly a suitcase.

"What's that?" Agnes asked.

"Stuff," Marion replied.

"What kind of stuff?" Agnes had not thought of a suitcase.

"Clothes, underwear, makeup, and, you know, *stuff*. I've been buying little bits since you told me about the idea. She can't arrive in Canada without *stuff*."

The Tannoy boomed out the imminent departure of the airport express bus. They hustled Dolly onto it. The bus pulled away almost immediately. Agnes ran beside it, waving to Dolly, who was crying openly now, but trying to smile. Then she was gone. Agnes walked back to Marion, wiping her eyes of the tears.

"You looked like a fuckin' idiot, running after that bus, Agnes," Marion said.

"Shut up, Marion," Agnes answered.

"Okay," came the usual reply. They linked arms and headed for home.

CHAPTER THIRTY-FIVE

It was 3:15 p.m. Agnes had already dressed Connie. And Marion looked beautiful in her lemon full-length dress. It had not been designed as a full-length, but it was now. They were sitting at the kitchen table, waiting for Agnes to emerge from her bedroom. Marion was bored waiting.

"Are you all right, Agnes?" she called.

"Coming, give me a second!" Agnes roared back.

Marion looked over at Connie. She was wearing a cream-and-cocoa suit Agnes had bought for her.

"You look lovely, Mrs. Reddin," Marion said, and Connie smiled back. Marion was just thinking that her comment had been wasted when Connie spoke.

"You do too, Marion." Marion sat open-mouthed at this. But Connie wasn't finished. "You have always been a good friend to Agnes. I forget so much, Marion, but I promise you, I will never forget that." Then the blankness returned to Connie's face. This was the first time Marion had ever experienced one of Connie's lucid moments and it scared the shit out of her.

Agnes emerged. A vision. The dress looked beautiful on the hanger, but now, wrapped around Agnes, it was positively divine.

"Right, then, let's go," Agnes said, and she led the trio down the stairs.

* * * * *

The horse and carriage that awaited Agnes the bride was surrounded by two crowds. One was the crowd of children awaiting
"grushie." This is an Irish custom of tossing a handful of coins to the
ground which the children would scramble to collect. It symbolizes,
it is said, the sharing of your good fortune with your neighbors. The
other crowd were all waiting to see would she do it, would she wear
"the dress." Here was a lot of chattering from the assembled women.
Across the street, in Cullen's Pub, even the men stood to look over
the window's half-curtain to see would this "young wan" defy the
church and go to the altar in white.

Marion was the first to emerge from the building. The horse exhaled noisily and adjusted his stance, making a *clip-clop* sound as he
transferred his weight from one hoof to another. A few women in
the crowd "oohed" and "aahed" at Marion's dress. She did a little
spin, smiling. She was delighted. Connie emerged from the building next and, shuffling past the still-spinning Marion, made her
way to Mrs. Delany, who was to escort her to the church. Then they
could hear the sound of Agnes' stiletto heels on the concrete steps.
This sent the crowd back to a hush. The footsteps got louder, and
then Agnes emerged from the darkened hallway onto the street.
The first reaction was a gasp at the beauty that emerged from the
building. Then came the buzz of reaction to what she was wearing.
She was wearing "the dress." But *what* a dress it was. The veil shimmered in the light breeze, the ancient pearls on the bodice sparkled
like diamonds as the sun shone across them, and the silk beneath
the Galway lace glowed like a warm beacon. Agnes stood there before her neighbors, glowing. She looked like an angel. The coins for
the grushie were held tightly in Agnes' hand. They were wet from
the nervous perspiration of her palm. She tossed them into the air,
and they fell to the ground like a shower of metallic snowflakes.

Nobody moved. The dress had them enraptured. The crowd just stood and looked in awe at this beautiful dress. Then someone began to clap. Agnes looked in the direction of the sound. It was Mrs. Cunningham, the butcher's wife. She called out, "Good on you, love, God bless the bride."

Agnes smiled to her. Then a few more joined in. It started as a small clatter of hands and built to a thunderous roar of applause. The children, awakened by the applause, suddenly dived onto the coins, and the crowd all laughed and cheered them on as they wrestled each other for the coins. Agnes climbed into the carriage beside Marion, and the crowd went quiet again.

A woman spoke from the crowd: "You've no man, love. You have no man to give you away," she called.

Agnes turned to her. "I just need a man to take me, I can give meself away."

And the crowd laughed again. The carriage pulled away to make the short two-hundred-yard journey to St. Jarlath's Church. It moved slowly. The crowd moved behind the carriage.

In the church, Redser Browne waited at the altar. He was shaking more from the coffee Tommo Monks had poured into him than from the nervousness of becoming a new groom. The church was already nearly full, and with the crowd coming behind Agnes added to that, it would be absolutely crammed. A few were there to see Redser and Agnes take their wedding vows, but most were waiting to see the priest turn the young wan away for wearing white while getting married "in sin." The debate was this: nobody was in any doubt that she would be turned away, it was just what way it would happen. Would he excommunicate her completely? Or would he just maybe send her away to change her clothes? They all waited.

In the front pew sat Constance, looking every inch the mother of the bride. She had a smile on her face, and her lips were moving slightly. She was either praying or talking to herself. It did not matter; nobody was paying a blind bit of notice to her.

In the vestry behind the altar, Father Pius was being dressed by two of the altar boys when the clerk came rushing in. His face was red and he was panting.

"She's on her way, Father," the clerk announced.

The priest looked into his face. He didn't have to ask the clerk the question; it was written in his expression.

The clerk nodded. "Yes, Father. She's wearing *the dress*," he said.

Father Pius closed his eyes. He finished dressing and instructed the altar boys to wait outside. When they were gone, he went and knelt before the statue of the Sacred Heart, Lord of All Mercy and Compassion, and he prayed to the Lord for forgiveness for what he was about to do.

Outside the church, Agnes stepped from the carriage. She had to wait a few moments until the crowd entering the church had cleared the doorway. When they were gone, she walked up the four steps and stood nervously in the huge Gothic doorway. Behind her, Marion was busy laying flat the now eight-and-one-half-foot train. Two Communion dresses and christening robes had taken their toll on the silk and satin train. Then Marion went to the church doors, opened them slightly, and peeked in. When she saw that the crowd had settled, she turned to Agnes, smiling, and winked.

"Ready?" she asked.

"Ready," Agnes answered and took a deep breath.

Marion waved at the organ player from the door. The pipe organ sounded a single note, and three seconds later, with Johnny Brennan pumping like a blacksmith's father, the organist struck up the "Wedding March." Two men held the doors open, and Marion entered first, smiling from ear to ear. With her head held high in the air, Agnes followed. As the doors closed behind them, they did not see the silver streak of the airplane passing overhead, bound for Canada, with Dolly aboard.

As the bridal group were walking up the aisle, Marion was receiving lots of congratulations and compliments on the beautiful flowers in the church, which had all come from her stall. As each comment came her way, Marion replied, "Thank you. The lilies are eightpence a bunch, the roses a shilling. I'm there all day tomorrow."

It seemed like a five-mile walk, but eventually Agnes arrived to stand beside her groom. They looked at each other.

"You look great," Redser said.

"You look like shit," Agnes replied through clenched teeth. He did; he was hung over. Agnes looked at Tommo, who was supposed to have been keeping Redser out of trouble. Tommo shrugged and hung his head. When the music finished, the couple stood waiting.

The vestry door clanked open and the altar boys entered, signaling the imminent arrival of Father Pius to the altar. The entire congregation stood. Father Pius walked onto the altar without so much as a glance at the bride and groom. He went and genuflected before the tabernacle containing the Host, and then turned. The congregation were supposed to sit now, but nobody moved. It was so quiet that even at the back of the church people could hear the rattle of Father Pius' rosary beads as he walked to the altar rails to meet Agnes and Redser. He stopped before them. He looked Agnes up and down.

"Agnes, do you know the church's ruling on proper dress for marriage in . . ." He searched. ". . . your situation?" he asked.

"Yes, Father," she answered. He looked at Redser, expecting a comment. Redser just looked blankly back at the priest and shrugged his shoulders.

"So why, then, do you come here in white?" Father Pius asked. Agnes began to answer but was interrupted from behind by her mother, who stood into the aisle to speak.

"That dress, Father, is the dress my mother was married in, it is the dress that I was married in, and today it is the dress that my daughter Agnes will be married in."

Throughout the church there was a collective intake of breath. Agnes turned, amazed, and looked in her mother's face. Her mother smiled at her. Father Pius stared at Connie, and she stared right back at him. After a couple of moments, he took away his gaze and looked to the ground. Everybody waited for his announcement. Instead Father Pius raised his arms and turned his palms upward.

"We are gathered here today in the sight of God to join together these two people in the Holy Sacrament of Marriage." In amazement, the congregation slowly sat down. This was indeed unbelievable.

Before Father Pius had gotten to the taking of the vows, the clerk was on the telephone giving the bishop a full account of the new priest's transgression. By the time Agnes and Redser were exchanging rings, Father Pius was out of a job.

As the happy couple left St. Jarlath's Church, there were great cheers. Handfuls of rice were thrown into the air and scattered across the churchyard. As the new Mrs. Agnes Browne climbed aboard the carriage, she was dripping with rice beads and trying to hold her husband erect. The carriage pulled away, the crowd followed, and soon the church was empty.

Empty except, that is, for Agnes' mother, Connie. She still sat in her seat, smiling. Father Pius saw her sitting there alone when he came out of the vestry. He walked down the steps and sat down beside her. They sat there next to each other in the quiet of the empty church, looking at the Holy Sacrament, and to the left the Virgin Mary, over to the right St. Christopher, beside him St. Jarlath.

"They are all here, all the saints." Father Pius spoke out loud with a little despair in his voice. "The place is full of saints, and yet there is no compassion." He wasn't moaning, he was just speaking his thoughts aloud.

"There was compassion here *today*," Connie said simply. The priest turned his head slightly to look at her. She was still smiling.

"You knew I'd do it, didn't you, Mrs. Reddin?" he asked her quietly.

"Yes, I did," she answered.

He turned his head away and exhaled as he spoke. "I had to," he said.

"Yes, you did, Father, you had to," Connie agreed.

They sat again in silence for a while. Then Connie opened her handbag and took a gold cross and chain from the inside pocket of it. She held it up. The sun was shining through the stained-glass windows, and the colors shimmered upon the golden crucifix.

"A young man gave me this—a long time ago, it seems. He said that if I ever needed anything from him I should just ask."

Father Pius looked at the twirling crucifix as if it were hypnotizing him. Constance leaned over and took the priest's hand. She turned it over, and into his palm she dropped the crucifix and chain. She stood up and looked down at the man, and again smiled. She stretched out her hand and gently stroked the side of his face.

"Paid in full, Michael. Paid in full," she said. He smiled, and closed his hand around the cross and chain that he had not seen in a long time. Connie began to walk down the aisle.

Father Pius stepped into the aisle and called after her. "Mrs. Reddin."

Constance stopped and turned to the young man.

"I can't explain how it feels when somebody saves your life," he said.

She held up her hand and smiled to him, and to the memory. "You don't have to explain to me, Michael. He saved mine too."

No, it's not the pixie dust, float-on-a-cloud, fairies-at-the-bottom-of-the-garden kind. But, oh God, yes! In the Jarro there is *magic*.